THE WIDOW'S
MATE

THE WIDOW'S
❧ MATE ❧

A Father Dowling Mystery

Ralph McInerny

St. Martin's Minotaur
New York

This is a work of fiction. All of the characters, organizations, and events portrayed in this novel are either products of the author's imagination or are used fictitiously.

www.minotaurbooks.com

Library of Congress Cataloging-in-Publication Data

McInerny, Ralph M.
    The widow's mate / Ralph McInerny.—1st ed.
        p. cm.
    ISBN-13: 978-0-312-36455-7
    ISBN-10: 0-312-36455-5
    1. Dowling, Father (Fictitious character)—Fiction.   I. Title.

PS3563.A31166W53 2007
813'.54—dc22

                                        2007014287

First Edition: August 2007

10 9 8 7 6 5 4 3 2 1

To Alice Osberger

For so much, for so long

❧ Part One ❧

Amos Cadbury had come to the St. Hilary rectory to advise Father Dowling on a matter of parish business, overriding the protests of the pastor.

"Amos, you must be the only lawyer in Fox River who makes house calls."

"Well, aren't you grateful," Marie Murkin fumed. Loyal as she was to Father Dowling, the housekeeper's regard for the patrician lawyer was on a very high level indeed.

"I am told the parish center is full of lovely widows," Amos said with a smile.

Marie was almost shocked. Amos had lost his wife ten years ago and, in a tasteful way, had been mourning her ever since. He always wore black; of course, most lawyers do, but Marie discerned continuing grief even in the lawyer's lighter moments. She approved of this. Even if he were younger than he was, it was unthinkable to Marie that Amos might have married again. There is monogamy and monogamy, and his, she was sure, was unaffected by the loss of his wife.

"Other than Marie?" Father Dowling asked.

This was too much. Marie glared at the pastor, turned on her heel, and stomped off to her kitchen. Seated at her table, a cup of tea before her, she resisted the thought that maybe Father Dowling's remark was not as facetious as it seemed. Was it possible that Amos Cadbury's frequent visits to the rectory were explained by . . .

She shook the thought away as unworthy, but even so there was the beginning of a wistful little smile at the corners of her mouth. Then another thought occurred.

Had Amos been serious in suggesting that the parish center was gaining a reputation as a kind of singles club for the elderly? Needless to say, Marie did not consider herself to be in the same age group as the denizens of the center, even though some were in fact younger than herself. The great difference was that she was still active, carrying on as she always had, whereas the men and woman who came to the center to while away the day playing bridge and shuffleboard or just reminiscing seemed all too content to find themselves in the twilight years of their lives. However that might be, it was equally true that pairings took place among them, stormy little romances, jealousies, competitions, smiles and tears. Like the pastor, Marie had been more amused by than disapproving of this belated resurgence of the attraction between the sexes. Edna Hospers, who directed the center, had another view.

"I found them necking in a classroom," she had said to Marie recently of one ancient couple.

"Necking?"

"What did you call it in your day?"

Thus was threatened what had begun as an uncharacteristically pleasant exchange with Edna. In her day? Marie rose from her chair, trying to conceal her wrath. What had promised to be a nice gossip about the old people had turned into Edna's suggestion that Marie was one of them.

Edna pretended not to notice the housekeeper's reaction. "Ever since the Widow Flanagan started coming here, the center has been absolutely electric with intrigue."

Marie sat again. "Really?"

"Half the other women shun her. They call her the Queen Bee. But they're all flirting like crazy now in competition with her."

This was more like it. Marie accepted a cup of coffee and adopted a receptive expression.

"Do you know her, Marie?"

"Melissa Flanagan? Oh, yes. It is an old parish family."

"Of course, she's younger than the others."

"Surely not by much."

"How old would she be?"

It was an opportunity not to be missed. "Not much younger than you."

There were those who complained of a loss of memory, but Marie was not among them. Father Dowling regarded her as a walking archive of parish history, and the fact was that she knew a lot more than was likely to end up in any archive. It almost surprised Marie herself how Melissa Flanagan's tragic history was suddenly vivid in her mind, but now was not the time to distract Edna with that story.

Edna laughed. "She could be my mother."

"She never had children."

"Part of it is that she is so much better off than the rest of them. I heard her telling our Lothario about a Caribbean cruise she had been on."

"Who is Lothario?"

Edna turned first east, then west in her desk chair. "Gregory Packer. You must have met him."

Marie looked closely at Edna to see if the remark meant more than it said. "The tall fellow?"

"With the wavy hair and the sparkling eyes. Contact lenses, I'm sure. Because of him and the Widow Flanagan, I am being turned into a chaperone. A duenna."

Marie had let it go. Edna was always improving her mind and was given to odd words from time to time. Gregory Packer was a sore subject to Marie. When he had come by the rectory kitchen a month ago to pay his respects, she made tea and offered him a slice of lemon meringue pie over his protests.

"You must have made that for the pastor."

"Of course I did. And all he would take is a sliver." Marie had put nearly a quarter of the pie on the dish she set before her guest.

"Is this your idea of a sliver?"

"Eat."

"You don't remember me, do you?"

Marie smiled. Gregory had been an altar boy in the days before Roger Dowling was named pastor of St. Hilary's. That was when the Franciscans had charge of the parish, a melancholy memory for Marie, who had never really gotten along with the friars.

In those days, altar boys had been dressed like little Franciscans, perhaps in the hope that they would consider a vocation. No one would have thought of Gregory as a future friar. He had been the terror of the parish school, forever on the carpet before the principal, but his misbehavior had somehow endeared him to those who had to scold him. Marie herself had once come to his rescue when one of the friars caught him drinking altar wine in the sacristy after Mass. Rather than empty the wine cruet into the sink, Gregory had tossed off the ounce remaining. The friar's outburst had brought Marie to the sacristy. Once the situation was clear to her, she took Gregory by the ear and marched him outside. Halfway to the house, she stopped and faced the culprit. What a good-looking lad he was. The twinkle in his eye suggested that he knew she had rescued him.

"It tasted awful," he said.

"Well, now you know."

She had taken him on to the rectory kitchen and given him a glass of milk to wash away the taste of the wine.

"You live right here?" he asked.

"I have an apartment in the back of the house. And my own staircase." It was not always clear to Marie that the parishioners understood that her quarters were sequestered from those of the priests.

"Are you some kind of nun?"

Marie was startled. "Do I look like a nun?"

He smiled. "No, you look like Ingrid Bergman."

How could she not like a boy like that? If Marie had had children, she would have had a son like Gregory, she was sure. No one's idea of a goody-goody, the sort of boy the friars favored, but a real boy. Of course, Marie looked nothing like Ingrid Bergman. Well, maybe a little . . .

Now, all these years later, Gregory had returned and was again seated at her kitchen table devouring the huge slice of lemon meringue pie she had put before him.

"So what brings you back to St. Hilary's?"

"I wanted to see you, for one thing."

Marie beamed. Surely she was justified in thinking that her long tenure as housekeeper had made her virtual pastor of the parish. Not that Marie was sympathetic with all this nonsense about ordaining women, but a housekeeper of the kind she was inevitably found herself engaged in a sort of pastoral activity. It was her practice to screen visitors, take them off to her kitchen, and find out why they had come. She told herself she was just trying to ease the burden on Father Dowling—not that he always appreciated her attempts to counsel visitors, but Marie knew she was helpful and did not repine when the pastor teased her about her efforts. Gregory's remark seemed confirmation of the influence she had.

"How long will you be in town?"

"Oh, I'm back for good." He grinned. "Well, anyway I'm back. Things have certainly changed around here. What's going on at the school?"

Marie explained to him that Father Dowling had turned the school into a parish center. "There weren't enough families with young children to keep up the school." No need to mention all the nuns who had gone over the wall.

"I saw a lot of people in the playground."

"Seniors," Marie explained.

"Maybe I'll look into it."

Marie laughed. "You're much too young for that."

"I'm in my fifties."

Marie let it go. No need to get into ages. The truth was that Gregory induced thoughts of a "September Song" romance.

"Do you still think I look like Ingrid Bergman?"

"I hope not. She's dead."

"You're not wearing a ring."

"Oh, I'm single." The way he said it suggested there was a story there. Marie settled into her counseling mood.

"Tell me about it."

"Not on the first date."

Honestly. Thank heavens Father Dowling couldn't hear her giggling.

Gregory finished his pie and pushed back from the table. "I shouldn't be taking up your time."

"You caught me in a free moment."

He stood. Marie resisted the impulse to tell him to sit down again. He had called this a first date—a joke, of course, but it suggested she would be seeing more of him. She found that she did not want to take him into the study and introduce him to Father Dowling. First she wanted to find out where he had been and what he had been doing since he left the parish. She remembered that he had enlisted in the navy. It seemed another bond, not that memories of the sailor Marie had married were happy ones.

Gregory had not returned. Then she had spotted him on the playground, at the center of a flock of cackling hens. Honestly. He noticed her and waved, but that was all. Marie felt jilted.

Then Edna told her of the swath Gregory was cutting through the women at the parish center. Lothario indeed.

"I'm surprised you let someone that young hang around here, Edna."

"He must be the same age as the Widow Flanagan. They seem to have known one another."

Again Marie resisted the urge to tell Edna the story of Melissa Flanagan. Of course Melissa would have known Gregory. Now that she thought of it, the two of them must have been in the same class in the parish school. When she did leave Edna, Marie went through the old gym that had been turned into a common room. At various tables, bridge games went on, some serious, some merely the occasion for companionship. Gregory was at a table with Melissa, just the two of them, and no cards in evidence. Melissa was smiling into Gregory's face as he spoke to her. It hurt a bit to see what a nice couple they made. Perhaps something would come of their reunion. With a resigned sigh, Marie pushed through the door and outside. The air was warm; there was a lovely scent of lilacs; birds twittered about. No wonder there was all that billing and cooing among the elderly. Edna might be impatient with it, but Marie walked back to the rectory in a wistful mood.

Her reverie was disturbed when Father Dowling appeared in the kitchen doorway. "Do you think you could scare up a little lunch for Amos and me? He's staying for the noon Mass."

Amos, too, came into the kitchen. "I offered to take him out to lunch, Marie. I hate to impose on you."

She shooed them off to the church and got to work. Scare up lunch indeed. She would show Father Dowling. Amos Cadbury, thank God, did not have the appetite of a bird, so feeding him was a challenge.

2

Amos Cadbury was surprised to see Melissa Flanagan in church for the noon Mass. What distracting memories she brought back. A long-ago meeting in his office with Luke Flanagan and his son, Wallace, was vividly before his mind. The result of that meeting had left Wallace and his wife, Melissa, financially comfortable, to put it mildly. Amos had been opposed to what father and son had come to do, but the two of them had made up their minds, and his demurrals went unheeded. No matter how much wealth old Flanagan transferred to his son, he might have been disowning him. Or perhaps vice versa.

'This is your idea," Wallace had said. "I just don't want to become a cement contractor."

Flanagan senior had made a fortune with his fleet of trucks that carried freshly mixed cement to building sites during the construction boom that had transformed downtown Fox River, and his prosperity had continued.

"What can you expect?" Luke Flanagan asked Amos. "He's a college graduate." He sounded as if he regretted the opportunities he had provided his son. He himself had not finished high school, going off with the Seabees before graduation and getting the experience that had enabled him to develop Flanagan Concrete into a lucrative business. Education or not, Amos considered Luke more intelligent than his son.

"What will happen to the business?" Amos asked in turn.

Luke looked gloomy. "I suppose I could sell it eventually. Or turn it over to my nephew Frank."

Frank Looney was everything Luke might have hoped for from his son. A diligent worker, he had begun driving one of the trucks, then moved into the office and soon was Luke's right-hand man.

"Going to Loyola didn't spoil him," Luke said.

In a few years, Frank was effectively running Flanagan Concrete, even though Luke still came to the office several times a week. There was something gratifying about watching his fleet of trucks set off, the great mixers mounted on them turning slowly, everything timed so that when they arrived at a building site, the cement would be ready to pour. But Luke had become a spectator of what he had created, and in time his nephew Frank succeeded him. The way things had turned out, Frank would have inherited Flanagan Concrete in any case.

Years in the law had prepared Amos for the unexpected in human behavior, but the disappearance of Wallace Flanagan had seemed incredible at the time, and even more incredible as it receded into the past.

Melissa had come to Amos with the news that she had not seen her husband for a week and had no idea where he might be.

"Has this ever happened before?"

"No!"

"Was there a quarrel?"

"We never quarreled."

That was possible, of course, but Amos considered it a pardonable exaggeration in the circumstances. With some reluctance he suggested that Wallace Flanagan's absence be reported to the police.

"I'ved hired someone to find him."

"You have!"

"A man named Tuttle."

Dear God. Amos wondered if Tuttle could find Flanagan even if the man weren't missing.

"I wish you had come to me first."

Her mention of Tuttle made Amos less reluctant to suggest that they check with the bank and Wallace's broker. If Wallace had decided to disappear, he had doubtless provided for his future. He might have cleared out with everything and left Melissa penniless. But the savings and investment accounts were unchanged.

"I thought Mr. Tuttle would tell you," Hibbs, the broker, said.

"You gave this information to Tuttle?"

Hibbs was surprised by Amos's indignation. He looked at Melissa. "Isn't he working for you?"

She nodded. Hibbs looked at Amos as if he expected an apology.

Melissa's two Flanagan sisters-in-law took turns staying with her during the weeks that followed. Tuttle sought an appointment with Amos but was refused. Amos might be the Flanagan lawyer, but he would have nothing to do with Tuttle. Then, years later, the suspense ended.

The body had been discovered when one of Flanagan's trucks had difficulty unloading its burden at a building site. The flow of cement had unaccountably stopped. The driver tried to get it going again, but unsuccessfully. He had to return to Flanagan's, several acres of land near the airport, pocked with excavations and with huge piles of sand and gravel and other ingredients of the company product. There was no choice but to wash out the contents of the mixer, and that was when the mangled body was found. It was removed in pieces. The left arm was intact, and there was a wedding ring that was the basis of identifying the body of Wallace Flanagan.

Melissa called Amos when the news was brought to her, and Amos went with her to McDivitt's Funeral Home, where McDivitt took Amos aside and advised against exposing Melissa to the horror of the remains. In the funeral director's office the ring was produced. Mellisa cupped it in the palm of her hand, staring at it, her calmness eerie. Then she held the ring up so she could read the inscription inside. She handed it to Amos. MELISSA AND WALLACE. 14.II.76. Amos could remember the wedding, performed by a trio of Franciscans at St. Hilary's Church. He stood and put his arm around Melissa, and finally she cried. He felt the shudder of her body beneath his arm; he and McDivitt avoided one another's eyes. Amos urged Melissa to her feet and led her outside. He held the door of the car open, but before she got in he handed her the ring. She looked at it almost in horror and shook her head. Amos had no choice but to put it into his pocket, get her settled, and drive off. On the way, he telephoned Luke Flanagan.

"Bring her to the house." Luke seemed relieved that Melissa had turned first to Amos rather than her father-in-law in her distress.

Melissa had continued to rely on Amos during the following

dreadful days. He made the arrangements with McDivitt and with the friars of St. Hilary's, making sure that the Flanagans were kept informed. Father Dowling was on retreat and Mrs. Flanagan, a Third Order Franciscan, wanted the friars. On the day of the funeral, Melissa insisted that Amos sit with her in the front pew. Luke was on the other side of the new widow, then his daughters, then Frank Looney. The ceremony had been penitential for Amos. The friars were in the grip of the new view that the departed could be assumed to be in heaven, even now enjoying the beatific vision. A funeral thus became an occasion for rejoicing rather than mourning, beaming faces, bouncy music, and, of course, eulogies afterward. The homily had already canonized Wallace Flanagan, but now a number of friends gave testimonials about the man whose remains—*membra disjecta*—were in the huge casket in the main aisle. Anecdotes, jokes—it might have been a roast, and then, thank God, one of the speakers broke down and wept. He could not finish what he had wanted to say and finally stumbled back to his pew. Amos learned afterward that his name was Gregory Packer. Outside the church, Amos went up to him and shook his hand wordlessly, but it was meant to thank him for the grief he had displayed. Packer seemed surprised. Then he grinned. "I don't know what got into me."

"Call it a human impulse. And a Christian duty."

Packer stared at him. Then once more that unsettling grin.

At the cemetery Amos mentioned it to Luke.

"He was a bad influence on Wally."

"At least he had the sense to weep at a funeral."

Luke shrugged his shoulders. "He was always putting ideas into Wally's head. Things might have been different if those two hadn't known one another."

Luke seemed to be suggesting that Packer had put the idea of giving up the family business into Wallace's head.

"Come to the house, Amos."

There were mountains of catered food, as well as Jameson's for the Irish, who knew what a funeral was for.

Melissa did not stay long and was soon convoyed away by classmates from Barat. Luke just shook his head when Amos produced the wedding ring. Amos put it back in his pocket and later into his office safe. Eventually, he was sure, Melissa would want to have it.

But the transfer had never been made. From time to time, Amos noticed the sealed envelope in his safe marked FLANAGAN WEDDING RING. Once he had taken it back to his desk, opened the envelope, and held the ring up to the light. That was when he noticed the legend on the outer surface of the ring. TILL DEATH DO US PART.

Amos shifted on his knees and managed to drive away these memories and attend to Father Dowling's noon Mass. Afterward, he returned with Roger Dowling to the rectory, where Marie first served an avocado salad that elicited Amos's praise.

"Avocado as in lawyer?" Father Dowling said. "This must be one of Marie's theme luncheons."

"I hope not," Amos said when the salad was followed by an omelet that melted on the tongue. "You can't make an omelet without breaking eggs. Is that another reference to my law practice?"

Marie ignored this, but she tuned in when Amos mentioned having seen Melissa Flanagan at the noon Mass.

"She's a frequent presence at the center," Marie said.

"At her age?"

"You'd be surprised." Marie did not say how.

Father Dowling said, "She tells me she has been traveling a lot and now wants to settle down."

"The Flanagans never really left the parish," Marie said.

"She's a widow, isn't she?" Father Dowling asked.

"Yes." Amos let it go at that. "Marie, you deserve a *cordon bleu.*"

"To go with her black belt?"

After lunch, Amos called his driver. Father Dowling came outside with him, and they waited for his car. On the playground, groups of the elderly were visible. It was difficult to think of Melissa Flanagan in such a setting.

Father Dowling sometimes thought that his friend Captain Phil Keegan regarded the baseball season as the secular equivalent of the liturgical year's Ordinary Time. Several times a week now, Phil came to the rectory to follow the fortunes of the Cubs. Even the smallness of Father Dowling's television screen no longer drew his complaints, but then baseball is a game that does not wholly absorb the attention of viewers. These were the occasions when the pastor of St. Hilary's was made privy to the current activities

of the homicide division of the Fox River police, of which Phil
was the head. It seemed the Pianone family was trying to buy
into Flanagan Concrete.

"How does that concern your department?"

"It doesn't, but old Luke Flanagan complained to Robertson
about it," Phil growled. Robertson, the chief of police, was a crea-
ture of the Pianones, whose influence in Fox River was pervasive.

"Hasn't Luke retired?"

"His nephew Frank Looney took over some years ago. Luke
might have been waiting for definitive news of what happened to
his son. I suspect the Pianones made Frank Looney an offer he
can't refuse."

Whatever the tainted sources of their money, the Pianones were
interested in concealing it with legitimate investments.

"They already have half the unions. I suppose that's their
wedge, the drivers."

"Is that a crime?"

Another growl. "Nothing will stay legitimate long if the Pianones are involved. They will soon be in control of all major
construction in Fox River."

It was Phil's cross to be running the one division of the police
force that wasn't under the Pianone thumb. Of course, he'd had
to accept Peanuts Pianone into his division, but Peanuts was regarded as too dim to be used by the family. Phil had agreed to
Peanuts as his insurance against any further Pianone incursion
into homicide. Into the investigating side of it, that is.

The young pitcher who had been part of the trade for Greg
Maddux was on the mound for the Cubs and hadn't allowed a hit

in four innings. Moreover, he had stroked a homer over the left field wall in the second, putting the Cubs ahead 1–0.

"And they said that without Maddux the Cubs were dead," Phil gloated.

Phil's remark about the Pianone control of the drivers at Flanagan Concrete disturbed Father Dowling. Earl Hospers, Edna's husband, had finally been released from Joliet, and he had found employment driving one of the Flanagan mixers. If the Pianones got involved in Flanagan's, it might be construed as a violation of Earl's parole. He asked Phil if that was possible.

"All he has to do is keep his own nose clean."

"I'm sure he'll do that."

Phil said nothing. Earl Hospers was something of a delicate subject. Phil had been involved in the arrest and conviction of Edna's husband, a case so complicated that it was difficult to prove that a murder had been committed. The only one who hadn't doubted Earl's guilt was Earl himself, and he would have felt unjustly treated if he had not been sent to Joliet as an accessory to manslaughter. He had been a model prisoner. Father Dowling had proposed to Edna that she turn the then empty parish school into a center for the increasing number of seniors in the parish, and during the long years of loneliness Edna had raised their children, made the center flourish, and remained loyal to her husband. Now they were reunited, and any possibility that their refound peace could be disturbed was bothersome.

"I wonder if I should mention this to Edna."

"I wouldn't."

Of course Phil wouldn't. Edna's not wholly reasonable resentment of Phil's role in Earl's misfortune had never gone away, and

Phil avoided Edna when he visited St. Hilary's, and vice versa. Father Dowling decided he would mention it to Edna. Perhaps he could devise some parish job for Earl to get him out of harm's way. He voiced the thought to Phil.

"This place will be crawling with parolees."

"What do you mean?"

"I understand that Gregory Packer has been attending the center."

"Packer!"

Phil looked at him. "You didn't know?"

Marie Murkin had appeared in the doorway of the study, bearing another bottle of beer for Phil. She was staring at him. "What was that about Gregory Packer?"

There were pastors who would have called this eavesdropping, but Father Dowling was not a stickler for protocol. Besides, Marie, for all her nosiness, was an invaluable asset to the parish. True enough, she sometimes acted as if the cardinal had assigned Father Dowling to St. Hilary's as her assistant, but this was a pardonable consequence of her sense of seniority. After all, she had already been housekeeper for some years when Roger Dowling became pastor. Her relief that the parish had finally been delivered from the Franciscans made her eager to tell Father Dowling stories about his predecessors, but he soon put a stop to that. Phil, of course, was not surprised by Marie's question.

Father Dowling asked her if she knew Gregory Packer.

"He came to see me."

"When was that?"

"You were busy at the time or I would have brought him in to meet you."

"Did he want to see me?"

"He didn't say. He was an altar boy here long ago."

Phil grunted. "Some altar boy."

"What do you mean by that?" Marie demanded.

"He's had a checkered career. He spent a few years in Joliet at public expense."

Marie dropped into a chair, her mouth open. "No!"

Phil was distracted by the game and leaned toward the set. A long fly to right nearly cleared the wall, but with a heroic effort the fielder climbed the ivy and caught the ball. Phil cheered. The no-hitter was intact. He reached for the beer that Marie still held, but she pulled it out of reach.

"Tell me about Gregory Packer," she demanded.

Phil seemed to have forgotten mentioning him, but Father Dowling was also waiting for him to speak. So Phil told them about the checkered career of Gregory Packer.

"Five years ago or so, he had been tending bar on the Near North Side in Chicago, and his employer accused him of increasing his salary by failing to put money in the cash register. He had fiddled with the gizmo that prints out bills for the customers— pretty ingenious—but then something made the night manager keep an eye on him. Not only was he undercharging for drinks, he was pocketing other receipts. The manager told the owner, they concentrated a camera on him, and when the thing went to court the trial was over almost before it began."

"When did he get out?"

"Early this spring. Cy Horvath had known the guy years ago, saw an item in the *Sun-Times*, and looked into it. He noticed him here a week or so ago."

Marie had given Phil his beer during his recital, but now she looked as if she wanted to take it back. She stood. "Why are you hounding him?"

"Hounding him?"

"Oh," Marie cried, throwing up her hands and hurrying back to her kitchen.

Phil looked at Father Dowling. "What's that all about?"

"Well, she said he was an altar boy here."

"He was, at the same time Cy was."

"Cy was an altar boy?"

"Why not?"

"No reason in the world. It's just that I never heard it before."

"Cy doesn't talk about Cy much."

"You said this embezzling took place in Chicago five years ago. Was that his first scrape with the law?"

"Well, it was his first conviction. He had been in the navy and was discharged in San Diego and stayed on. Women liked him, and he seems to have been a kind of gigolo. But then a complaint was filed. He was accused of writing checks on a lady friend's account, a widow who owned the driving range he managed."

"And?"

"She withdrew the complaint when he proposed marriage."

"Did he marry her?"

"Yes." Phil sipped the beer, his eye on the screen. "A civil ceremony."

"And?"

"Oh, she divorced him. Got a court order to keep him away from her. That's when he came back to Chicago and got the job tending bar."

Sounds in the hallway indicated that Marie was listening in.

Father Dowling raised a hand and nodded toward the door. Phil understood. Not that he wanted to go on talking about Gregory Packer. In the eighth inning, a grounder scooted by the second baseman, and the batter was safe on a close call at first.

"Damn," Phil commented.

When Phil Keegan told Cy Horvath of Marie Murkin's reaction to learning about Gregory Packer, there was no alteration of expression on the lieutenant's Hungarian countenance. Telling Phil that he had known Greg Packer when they were altar boys at St. Hilary's had been meant to explain why he had checked on Greg, but Phil seemed to find nothing odd about his curiosity. The truth was that the memory of Greg had been playing at the edges of Cy's mind for years, ever since the gruesome killing of Wally Flanagan. Wally, too, had been an altar boy, and he and Greg had been thick as thieves until Greg went off to the navy, and they had all been infatuated with Melissa. It was in the hope of getting a glimpse of her that Cy had driven out to St. Hilary's and parked on the street next to the school and waited. He had learned from Luke that she was back in the parish, living in the family home Luke had turned over to her when he rented a retirement apartment near the Magnificent Mile.

"What's she doing now?"

"She likes that parish center Father Dowling started. I went there just once. Bunch of old bastards reliving their lives."

"Why would Melissa like a center full of seniors?" She was Cy's age.

"I never did understand that woman."

So Cy had driven out there and parked and, sure enough, caught a glimpse of Melissa. She was as beautiful as ever. He immediately recognized the guy she was with, too. Greg Packer. Cy had thought Greg was still in Joliet. He must be the reason Melissa liked the center, but neither of them was in the age group of the people that hung around there. Seeing the two of them invited him to put two and two together in a way all his police training warned against, but he couldn't help it. Nor could he help thinking of the person missing from that scene, Wally Flanagan.

More murders go unsolved than are ever solved, of course, and in Fox River there were investigations that ran into the protective net with which politicians had surrounded the Pianones. If the body in the cement mixer had been anyone other than Wally Flanagan, a possible Pianone connection would have been Cy's first thought, but that made no sense. Wally had been set free by his father when Luke turned over to him years in advance what he would have inherited. Wally had no interest at all in the cement business that explained all the money he received. So he had bought a membership in a brokerage firm, Kruikshank and Sharpe, and soon became the hotshot of the office. In a few years, he set himself up as an independent financial counselor and went about enriching his clients and adding to his own wealth.

During that period, Cy had seen Wally only once, in a Loop bar where he had stopped after checking something out with Chicago homicide. His old friend had exuded prosperity, but what they had in common was the fact that they had been kids together.

"Missie wants to move into the old parish, Cy." He meant Melissa.

"It's changed."

"Of course it's changed. Everything changes." He looked almost glum when he said it. "So what are you doing?"

Cy told him.

"Hoping to last long enough to get your pension? Listen, Cy, let me have a thousand and I'll get a portfolio started for you. Add regular amounts and I all but guarantee you your retirement will come years sooner and be a helluva lot more comfortable."

In those days, the thought of handing over a thousand dollars to start an investment portfolio had all the never-never quality of winning the lottery. Cy told Wally he would think about it.

"Don't forget, I have a lot of concrete experience." He punched Cy's arm to make sure he got the joke.

That's when the blonde joined them. She was tall and suited and gorgeous, and only an idiot would doubt that something was going on between the two.

"This is Sandy," Wally said. He added, "Another client."

Sandy laughed. Cy got out of there. In his line of work, nothing surprised him much, but the idea that the man who had won Melissa would fool around with even a dish like Sandy almost shocked Cy. Of course he remembered the woman when Wally disappeared. During the investigation, he got access to Wally's office records and identified her. Sandra Bochenski. When he went to her address, a posh apartment house on the North Shore, he learned that she had moved.

The manager, an officious little guy named Ferret with a cookie-duster mustache, had been eager to talk about the former tenant. "My God, she was something. When a Polack is beautiful there is absolutely nothing like it." He paused. "You Polish?"

"Hungarian."

He seemed relieved. Cy showed him a photograph of Wally. Ferret nodded. "Sure, that's her fiancé."

"What happened?"

"What do you mean?"

"Well, she moved away."

"They were going to settle on the West Coast."

"She told you that?"

"Look, she always stopped to talk. Real class." Ferret looked around. "Most of the residents are a pain in the whatchamacallit. Expect me to tug my forelock when they go by. Not her. And generous? A huge tip every Christmas."

"How long did she live here?"

"Just a couple years. But I knew her better than many who have been here forever."

"Where on the West Coast?"

"California." He thought. "I think San Diego."

Cy decided not to tell Ferret that Wally's wife in Fox River had reported him missing. He made inquiries, but no Wallace Flanagan was listed in the San Diego directory. One of the problems Cy faced was what Wally could be charged with when he was found. As far as Melissa could tell, he had left all their money behind, so if she was abandoned she certainly wasn't destitute. Of course, if Wally married Sandra Bochenski he would be committing bigamy, but when was the last time a bigamist had been put away? It was the affront to his personal memories rather than the criminal code that made Cy wish he could haul Wally in.

Because of the personal connection, he might have stayed on it, but one case gets pushed aside by later ones; he had less and less time to devote to the mysterious disappearance of Wally Flanagan. Frank Looney was no help.

Frank spent a lot of time in the yard and had a dusty look. He shook his head. "Know what I remember? He said more than once, 'I wouldn't be caught dead in this place.' I love it."

"Did you see much of him?"

Frank shook his head. "It broke my uncle's heart when Wally told him there was no way he would take over the business. Lucky break for me, of course. I don't know when I stopped worrying that Wally would change his mind and Uncle Luke would tell me the deal was off."

Talking with Melissa was the hardest thing of all.

"We were altar boys together." A dumb opening, but why not.

"I remember." Her hair was so black she looked more Spanish than Irish, and the olive skin added to the impression. Her eyes were green, so his memory had not played him false.

"Melissa, I have to ask you. Did you have any intimation that he would leave?"

"Why would he leave? Cy, it must be amnesia. You read of cases like that." She shivered. "Imagine not knowing who you are."

"No money problems?"

"Only that we had too much."

Of course, he did not tell her of meeting Sandy or the possessive way she had taken Wally's arm, and why tell her of the number of people who just disappear and are never located? Maybe she was right and it was amnesia. In a way, that made it more likely Wally would be found. He would seek help, trying to find out who he was. Cy wished he hadn't encouraged Melissa to think that. She reached out and laid a long-fingered hand on his arm.

"Of course you're right. I hired a lawyer."

"Isn't Amos Cadbury the family lawyer?"

"I couldn't ask him to do this."

"Who'd you hire?"

"A man named Tuttle."

Cy had made no comment. Tuttle! Now, years later, he thought of the time line since Wally disappeared. Ten years afterward, his body had been discovered in one of the Flanagan cement mixers. That seemed to put an end to it. The investigation had been intense but brief and was soon pushed aside by other matters. Cy had noticed Greg Packer at the funeral and had decided against talking to him. So once more, the waters of forgetfulness had closed over the mystery. Now, half a dozen years later, Melissa was living in the Flanagan house in St. Hilary's parish, a frequent presence at the senior center, and Greg Packer, a graduate of Joliet, had reappeared, and the two seemed to have formed a pair.

5

If Tuttle had been in the habit of remembering his mistakes, hiring Hazel would be at the top of the list. She had come to his office as a part-time temp because he couldn't afford a full-time secretary, and she had stayed on. Her motive could not have been security, at least employment security. She had learned Tuttle wasn't married, and apparently the prospect of running his life twenty-four hours a day appealed. The thought of marriage terrified Tuttle, and the prospect of being tied to Hazel only increased the terror. That pitfall had been avoided. Tuttle was sure that his sainted parents had interceded for him and kept him single. The worst of it was that Hazel had vetoed Peanuts Pianone's hanging around the office.

"He's a professional asset," Tuttle had complained.

"What profession?" Hazel always sat erect at the computer, with her shoulders thrown back. She was a lot of woman.

He explained to her that Peanuts was a cop and kept him informed on what was going on at headquarters. No need to mention that his friendship with Peanuts cut his expenses since they usually drove around in the unmarked car Peanuts had been given to keep him on the move and out from under Captain Keegan's feet.

"What's he done for you lately?"

If Hazel thought Peanuts destroyed what little class Tuttle's office had, Peanuts hated her guts. Once the two friends had whiled away hours in Tuttle's office—Chinese or Italian food sent in, a couple of beers, a little nap afterward. In retrospect, those times could seem like heaven to Tuttle. Peanuts never had much to say, but he listened while Tuttle constructed a narrative of his life that made him seem less of a loser. Hazel had destroyed all that.

"Get rid of her," Peanuts muttered.

"I owe her too much back salary."

"Let her sue."

"I could act as her lawyer."

"You want me to take care of it?"

Peanuts had droopy lids, but his little agate eyes gleamed. It took a minute before Tuttle understood what Peanuts was suggesting. They never talked of the Pianone family, of course; it was too dangerous to know much about what Peanuts's relatives were up to. Once early on, Peanuts offered to direct a little family business Tuttle's way, and a great inner moral drama went on in the lawyer's soul. He was saved only by the benign expression on his father's face in the photograph on his desk. Tuttle senior had encouraged his son during the long march through law school, during which Tuttle took every class at least twice. Measured by the clock, he might be the best-educated lawyer in town, not that he remembered much from law school. On graduation, his father had ponied up the money for this office, and on the door was painted TUTTLE & TUTTLE, a tribute to his father. He told Peanuts his strengths might not match the Pianone needs. Peanuts let it go. He probably couldn't have delivered anyway. Now there was a thought. What if Tuttle had decided to sell his soul and there was no taker?

"Forget about Hazel, Peanuts. She's a pain in the neck, but so what?"

"Why have a pain in the neck?"

He found himself singing Hazel's praises. She ran the office like a boot camp, but she had her good points. He tried to think of one.

This conversation took place when Peanuts was driving him back to the office after a long lunch at the Great Wall of China.

"She wouldn't know what hit her."

"Peanuts, please. Forget it. I'll forget we ever had this conversation."

What would Hazel think if she knew he had been pleading for her life? The elevator in his building was still on the blink, and Tuttle was huffing and puffing when he got to his floor. Outside the office, he stood a minute, getting his breath, and looked at the legend on the door. TUTTLE & TUTTLE. It failed to provide the usual sense of satisfaction. Was it for this that his father had sacrificed and he himself had spent all those years in the classroom? Tuttle sent up a little prayer to his father, who had died a week after Tuttle had finally managed to pass the bar exam, his sleeves full of notes, looking over the shoulder of the hotshot in front of him to see if they were answering questions in the same way.

He pushed open the door, then almost backed into the hallway again when Hazel greeted him with a big smile.

"I called the Great Wall." The smile gave way to a more familiar glare. "Is your cell phone on?"

"What's up?"

Hazel tore a page from a pad and thrust it at him. "I told her you'd meet her at this address."

"Who is she?"

"She wants a lawyer, that's the main thing." Hazel paused, looking reflective. "I could come along."

"And leave the office untended?"

He said it with feigned disbelief. Even so, she didn't have to laugh like that.

Chicago brought back so many things that Sandy Bochenski had shut out of her mind during the years in California. The past sticks to the places where it happened. All you do is add water, and long-ago things are present again. Water as in tears.

She had arranged for a room in the Whitehall over the Web and went there by cab from O'Hare. After a nap, she got into a sweat suit, laced up her tennies, pulled on a baseball hat, and set out. She told herself it was just her daily run, keeping to the schedule she'd been on for years, but this run had a destination. All she wanted to do was go by the building where she'd had the apartment, where her affair with Wally turned into their common desire to make it permanent. She jogged in place on the sidewalk across the street from the building. It might have been only yesterday that she had lived there. Suddenly she brought her arm over her mouth to stifle a sob. Passersby glanced at her, although joggers were normally invisible to the workaday world. Sandy regained her composure and then returned to the Whitehall, almost sprinting. In her room, she made the call to Tuttle, the lawyer.

His name had become familiar to her when she scanned Chicago papers for some clue to why Wally had not joined her. After several confusing days, she had called Wally's office, and a bright mindless voice cried, "Flanagan Investments! Your call is important to us. Please hold." She hung up. But she called again. On the third try, she held and then asked for Mr. Flanagan.

"Who should I say is calling?"

She returned the phone to its cradle. Was he there? The image of him in his office conducting business as usual while she waited like a fool in San Diego, expecting him to leave all he had and join her in California . . .

She bought Chicago papers; she did not know why. What did she expect to find, an apology from Wally? It was only weeks later, on a Web site, that she came upon an item telling of the disappearance of Wallace Flanagan. Her heart leapt. He was coming to her after all. For some reason, he had decided that he must cover their tracks decisively. But he was on his way, she was sure of it.

His wife had hired a lawyer named Tuttle to look into the mystifying disappearance of her husband. Sandy read the stories with a smile. Wally had left his wife wealthy; there was no reason for him to leave; there must have been foul play.

Whatever comfort she had derived from this development turned into deeper disappointment when days and weeks and then months passed and Wally did not join her, did not call or send any message. Sandy felt as deserted as Wally's wife. Not as well off, of course, but Wally had contributed to Sandy's portfolio, which under his direction had doubled in value.

Sorrow gave way to anger, even rage, and then subsided. Wally had made a fool of her, and there was nothing to be gained from brooding on it forever. Her self-esteem returned. She remembered that she was an attractive young woman and had the wherewithal to lead a carefree life. Vegetate in the California sun? After a few months of it, she longed for some purpose in her life, so she enrolled in a business course, suppressing the thought that knowledge of financial matters would be a link to Wally. There was a practical purpose; she intended to nurture her own investments, using an online broker. Another thought to be suppressed: She would make her money into a golden mountain, and somehow that would show Wally. Then she met Greg Packer.

He had been studying a bulletin board in the hallway when she came out of class, and he turned from it and stopped her. "Are you a student here?"

She might have ignored him, but his smile was disarming, and he was good-looking.

"Why do you ask?"

"I was thinking of taking a course. Look, where can we have coffee?"

Just like that. But why not? He was a potential fellow student. It felt good to be consulted about the courses. They went to the Starbucks up the street and sat at an outside table. She noticed that he did not have the mandatory California tan. She commented on it.

"I've only been here a few days."

"Where are you from?"

He brought out cigarettes and then paused. "Do you mind?"

"I'll join you."

"I'm from the Chicago area."

He was lighting her cigarette. "You came to stay?" She exhaled the question with the smoke.

"That depends." He sat back and looked around with contentment. "You natives have no idea how wonderful all this seems."

She did not correct him. He had taken a brochure from the rack by the bulletin board, and they began to talk about the courses.

"What are you taking?"

She told him.

"I wonder if I could sit in to see if I could handle it."

"Well, I can't give you permission, but I don't see why not."

"When is the next class?"

"Wednesday." It was a Monday. "It starts at three."

"Can we get anything to eat here?"

"Not a meal."

"Where do you suggest?"

She couldn't believe it. Half an hour later, they were sitting across from one another in a Mrs. Paul's, and she was telling him all about life in California. She had felt like a recruiter for the school; now she felt like someone from the tourist bureau. He seemed to get better-looking all the time, and he clearly found her attractive—and, after all, this was California. He appeared to think it was perfectly natural for two attractive strangers to be having dinner together an hour after they had first met.

She said, "Tell me about Chicago."

"You wouldn't like it."

Again she failed to mention that she, too, came from Chicago. What would he say if he knew she was almost as much of a newcomer as he was? A week later, when she told him, she approached the subject indirectly, asking if he knew *The Great Gatsby*.

"Tell me."

So she told him how Nick Carraway had felt when, new in West Egg, he had been asked directions, the questioner conferring on him the freedom of the neighborhood.

"I don't get it."

"I'm almost as new here as you are."

"Come on. I don't believe it."

What a lovely smile he had. Once she fessed up, the fact that they were both from Chicago was a bond. They went on a picnic on the shore below San Juan Capistrano. Sandy had bought a car, a convertible. As they lounged on their blanket, he watched an elderly couple go down to the water hand in hand, in swimsuits.

"Nobody grows old here," he said wonderingly.

He turned toward her, his face inches from hers, his eyes full of his dreamy thought. She leaned toward him and kissed him on the forehead.

She would never forget afterward that she was the one who had turned their casual friendship into something else. She seemed to be punishing Wally, but that was not the whole of it. Greg accepted her kiss without comment, then put his hand behind her head and pressed his lips to her forehead.

"You said the Chicago area," she said.

"Did you ever hear of Fox River?"

Her breath caught, but she managed to say, "I think so."

"Beyond the western suburbs."

"Oh, sure." She got out her cigarettes. She was smoking again now. "My broker came from there. His office was in the Loop, but he was a native of Fox River."

"No kidding."

"Tell me about Fox River."

"It would take about a minute. What was his name?"

The first time she said it, her voice was a whisper, and that was all wrong. "Flanagan."

"Wally Flanagan?"

"Don't tell me you know him!"

"We grew up together!"

"Do you see him often?"

He shook his head. "How many kids you went to school with do you still know?"

"But you remembered his name."

"We were altar boys together."

She laughed. He watched her as she did. She stopped. "I'm sorry. I just can't imagine the two of you as altar boys."

"I can still say the Latin prayers."

He proved it.

"I'm Catholic, too."

"With a name like Bochenksi, of course."

Another link, another bond. What if the affair with Wally and colluding with him to betray his wife had been a providential plan to get her to California where she could meet Greg? It was a nice thought that God was looking out for her. The next Sunday, they went to Mass together. Neither of them went to communion, and several days later Sandy went to confession and poured out her story. When she received absolution, she felt that she was finally rid of the self that had been in love with Wally Flanagan. The next time they went to Mass together, they both went forward with the communicants. Kneeling beside him afterward, her face in her hands, she thanked God for bringing her Greg Packer.

He had sat in on the class, and then he registered, so they studied together, and he marveled at how easily she picked up information on investments. She was about to tell him of her portfolio, of her motive for taking the course, but she didn't. The way she felt about Greg now, it would have seemed like a bribe. How chaste they were. It was perfect. It was how it should be. She had no hesitation in inviting him to dinner at her apartment.

"Wow," he said, looking around.

"You like it?"

"What are you, an heiress?"

"Ha."

He told her he was an orphan; she told him her own condition was not much better. Her affair with Wally had erected a huge barrier to her past, and she had stopped seeing her widowed father, who was the only close relative she had.

"Who will give you away?"

She looked at him. He waited. "Someone already has."

"Who?"

"Me."

"To whom?"

"You."

So three months after her arrival in San Diego, she became Mrs. Gregory Packer. They honeymooned in Taos. When they returned, he got a job managing a driving range.

"You can be the financier," he said.

By then, she had told him of her portfolio, of course. How ironic that it provided the security for their marriage—all those investments she had made under Wally's direction that were to have been the financial foundation on which she and Wally would build their life together.

"I feel like a gigolo."

"No you don't." And she tickled him.

Two years later she would look back on that idyllic period when she and Greg were newlyweds with awed horror. She came to regret telling him of her investments.

"Wally sure set you up," he said.

At the time, it didn't occur to her that she had never told him about her affair. She had described Wally as her broker. Even so, it was the first seed of doubt.

Greg became obsessed with her investments. The first time he suggested that the portfolio should be in both their names, an awful doubt began in her. His behavior increased the doubt. Her refusal made him surly and then abusive. After the first time he actually hit her, she locked him out of the apartment. Of course, he had a key, but that could not remove the chain and inside bolt. He beat on the door, and she covered her ears. It was awful. She was frightened of him now, truly frightened. She had never before been struck by a man, and this was her husband. When the noise stopped and he went away, she sat in an unlit room and asked herself what kind of an idiot she was. First she had been betrayed by Wally, and now she had married a monster who had been a boyhood friend of Wally's. Some hours later, when she was packing his things, determined that she would never again be exposed to Greg's abuse, she found the folder of clippings from Chicago papers. She sat on the bed and went through them. They were all about Wally and his disappearance. Sandy stared unseeing at the wall. Suddenly all the events of her meeting Greg took on a new and sinister aspect: their seemingly accidental meeting, their swift courtship, his interest in her investments. The worst thought of all was that Wally had told Greg of her. Had he suggested that Greg might play the role meant for him?

At two in the morning, she left the apartment, making two trips to her car in the garage below the building. As she put things in the trunk, she could scarcely breathe, half fearing that Greg would leap out from behind a parked car, but she got away and drove to Anaheim, where she stayed in a motel. The next day she sold her car and bought another and then drove north to Oxnard. The main thing was to sever all ties with the man she had married. She thought of using her mother's maiden name, but it was easier, if risky, to resume her own. How like Wally she had become.

As the years passed, Sandy felt she was putting in time in purgatory. No one who knew her would have understood. She began as a secretary in a brokerage and swiftly moved up the ladder. She had the Midas touch, and with respect to her own investments, it seemed almost a curse. The thought that amassing money was a silly objective would have been heresy in her Oxnard firm. Her marriage to Greg came to seem an unreal interlude. She did not divorce him, of course; that would have brought them together again. Wally? He, too, became a distant memory. Sometimes she thought that she had become a kind of nun. Religion had become her main consolation.

From time to time, she bought a Chicago paper, but she learned of Wally's death and the discovery of his body in one of the cement-mixing trucks his father owned from a news site on the Web. She might so easily never have learned of it. When she did, the kind of thoughts she had had when she discovered all the clippings about Wally that Greg had collected began again, more sinister still. Those thoughts would not go away. Of course, she had read of Greg's difficulties with the woman who owned the driving range he managed. The difficulty was smoothed over when he married her, making him a bigamist. From time to time, she ran a check on Greg, using Lexus, but his name never came up in connection with Wally's death. Greg's conviction for stealing from his Loop employer seemed in character. After he completed his term in Joliet, he no longer figured in Lexus.

But the discovery of Wally's body, nearly ten years after he disappeared, created the greatest mystery of all. What had he been doing during all those lost years? Why had he not joined her in San Diego? Not even time could make the hurt of his abandonment of her go away. So she had returned to Chicago.

Tuttle's secretary suggested that the lawyer come to her, and she named a coffee bar in Water Tower Place.

7

After all the years as a single mother, Edna found adjusting to Earl's release from Joliet difficult. So did he. Each of them had become used to life without the other, to solitude. Her work at the St. Hilary senior center, begun as a kind of therapy, had become a welcome and satisfying daily routine. Earl got a job as a driver for Flanagan Concrete and began the slow recovery from years of confinement. He tried to tell her what being free meant. She listened and had some inkling of the contrast. He could actually live his life as he wanted. What he wanted was to be with her and the kids, and a routine; the job at Flanagan's provided that. It sounded boring to Edna, but what did her job at St. Hilary's seem to him?

A remark of Marie Murkin's made her realize that Earl was working for a company connected with the Queen Bee, the Widow Flanagan, and until she learned that Melissa had no involvement in the company, Edna kept aloof from the dazzling new addition to her wards. Of course, the man she called Lothario, Greg Packer, kept the Queen Bee busy. When Marie told Edna the story of Melissa's husband, Edna felt a surge of sympathy for the attractive and still youthful widow. She supplemented Marie's knowing remarks with a study of back issues of the *Tribune*.

When she talked to Earl about it, he fell silent. "Don't get too curious," he advised.

"What do you mean?"

"It's a variation on the concrete overcoat."

She didn't understand. He explained, cryptically. The mob? Of course, she had heard of the Pianones. They were part of local lore, but it had always seemed a romantic exaggeration to Edna. She had even met Peanuts Pianone, the member of the family who was on the police force and always hanging about with Tuttle. Suddenly Melissa became for Edna a tragic and fascinating person, but it was rare when she found her apart from Greg Packer. She asked her to come up to her office for tea.

"This was the principal's office," Melissa said, standing in the doorway. "Sister Ellen Joseph."

"You went to school here?"

"A long time ago."

"I wouldn't have thought that possible. When was that?"

Melissa lowered her head and smiled. "You can't expect me to answer that."

Melissa marveled at the fact that Edna actually brewed tea, no tea bags.

"This tea set was a wedding gift."

"So you're married?"

"Oh, yes."

Edna wondered what the old people made of her. They would have known of her kids, of course, but for years there had been no husband in evidence. Earl's return had given her an advantage over Melissa but did not alter her sense that the two of them had known difficulties most women are spared.

Melissa tasted her tea and looked around the office. "How nice it must be to work here."

"I like it."

"But all us old people."

Melissa did show age, up close, but this did not alter her beauty.

"You and Greg Packer must be the youngest of those who come regularly."

"Are you fishing for my age?" She asked it with a smile. Edna knew her age, though. It seemed an unfair advantage to know as much about Melissa as she did, but how many people have their troubles trumpeted by the media, not once but twice?

Edna learned that Melissa and Greg had been students in the parish school at the same time. "My husband, too."

When the conversation was brought to the point that Edna had hoped for, she found she could not pursue it. "And you remained in the parish."

"Well, I'm back. My father-in-law didn't want to sell the family home when he moved to Chicago and suggested I take it."

"And you did?"

"Sometimes I regret it. All the memories."

Again Edna would have liked Melissa to pour forth those memories, and again she did not pursue it. Perhaps, when they got to know one another better, Melissa would tell her—but her own curiosity repelled her. How would she have reacted if people had pressed her on what had happened to Earl? "It bothers me that there is really so little for people to do in the center. If you have any ideas . . ."

"Don't change a thing! It's perfect as it is. There is more than enough to do, but it is just being here that is the main thing."

It was odd to think of this lovely woman with all the money in the world describing the Spartan offerings of the St. Hilary parish center as perfect. Edna was pleased. It confirmed her belief, born of experience, that the elderly did not want to be organized and hustled about and entertained. Bridge, shuffleboard, and mainly conversation, the exchange of memories and gossip, were entertainment enough.

"I feel I've had an interview with Sister Ellen Joseph," Melissa said when she finished her tea.

"Did that ever happen?"

"Oh, Greg Packer had more experience of that. He was the class rowdy." She said it with a burst of affection.

"Have you two kept in touch over the years?"

"Oh, no! He just popped up out of the past. I didn't really remember him. He didn't like that."

"Men are vain," Edna said, accompanying Melissa to the door.

"Like women."

It seemed a gentle scolding.

That first tête-à-tête left Edna full of admiration for Melissa Flanagan. She never referred to her as the Widow Flanagan again. The total absence of self-pity stirred Edna's sympathy. Melissa, she felt, was a kindred spirit.

8

Father Dowling got the story of Melissa Flanagan's husband from Marie, from Amos Cadbury, and from Phil Keegan, and the result made him ponder the nature of history. Accounts of the past are always built up from such sources. Marie was the perceptive onlooker, Amos had been a participant, and Phil represented the official, impersonal point of view. There were also the newspaper accounts, the least reliable of all because of their pretense to being neutral dispatches from outer space. He had been brought photocopies of these by Bill Kenner, a parishioner and longtime editor of the *Fox River Tribune*.

"It's all on the Web," he had said when Father Dowling first asked if the Flanagan case had been a big story.

"I don't use a computer."

Kenner sighed. "I envy you. The damned thing has ruined journalism. We're doomed anyway, you know. Circulation dwindles because any idiot with a computer has instant access to raw news twenty-four hours a day."

"The newspaper business has changed during your time?"

"Changed!" Kenner was a spindly man with gray hair that sat

on his head like a doily and brown eyes that seemed to emerge from purplish pockets. His mustache looked like an oversight, but he was constantly stroking it with thumb and index finger. His anger softened. "Father, did you ever see a linotype machine?"

"I don't believe I have."

"Oh, you couldn't now. They've all gone to wherever linotype machines go when they die. It was a lovely machine. Whenever I regretted going into journalism, I would go down and watch the linotype operators. It's all computerized now. Including the prose. No one has to know how to spell anymore. The computer does it for you."

There was more. They were seated on one of the benches that lined the walks of the parish grounds that led to the church or the school, this one in the shade outside the sacristy door. Kenner had not yet handed over the large envelope he had brought for Father Dowling, which looked crammed full. It seemed only fair to let him lament the changes in his profession. Kenner was in his early sixties and like some priests of that age apparently thought that the golden age in which he had begun had been replaced by one of lead—or of the plastic computers are housed in.

"But I'm raving." Actually Kenner spoke in the measured dirgelike tones of a sincere mourner.

"Didn't Mark Twain have something to do with the linotype?"

"The poor devil backed a rival that couldn't compete with it. He lost his shirt. Imagine, he began setting type by hand and ended wanting to mechanize the process."

Kenner fell silent as if, like the seminary chaplain, he had just announced a point for meditation and long thoughts were called for. Then he straightened on the bench and began to beat his knees with the envelope he had brought. "It's all here. Strange case."

"So it seems. From what I've heard. That's why I wanted the newspaper accounts."

"All the news that's fit to print."

"What do you mean?"

"The reported story is only the tip of the iceberg."

Father Dowling waited.

"Freedom of the press? Ha. People talk as if newspapers were owned by the public. They're private enterprise, Father, and they subsist on advertising and local support, generally. Of course, all that introduces constraints. College journalists regularly complain because the administration, which owns the student paper, exercises restraint. They seem to think this is a violation of the divine order of things. Wait until they get a real job."

"Your advertisers interfere?"

"Oh, they don't have to. We anticipate their interference. This story should tell you what I mean."

Kenner actually looked over both shoulders and leaned toward Father Dowling. He whispered the word. Had the four syllables of the name ever been enunciated more distinctly? "Pi-a-no-ne."

"Ah."

"After you read this stuff, if you want to talk about it, let me know."

They parted, and Father Dowling went back to the rectory and his study. He put the envelope in a desk drawer, lest it draw the curiosity of Marie Murkin. No need to tell her that he wanted to learn as much as he could of the strange events that had involved parishioners of St. Hilary's. All the more so now that Melissa Flanagan had become a regular at the parish center. Thus far, his meetings with her had been brief and ceremonial, the pastor acknowledging the return to the parish of an old parishioner. Perhaps he seemed a novelty to her. Her memories would be of Franciscans.

Nothing in her manner would indicate that she had been through such a series of horrible events. Father Dowling had detected in the accounts of the disappearance of Wally Flanagan the scarcely concealed suggestion that one more disgruntled spouse had decided to light out for the territory (he was rereading *Huckleberry Finn*). Accounts of the frantic wife's speculations as to what dreadful things must have happened to her husband, enclosed in double quotation marks, underlined the skepticism with which the jaded media regarded her explanations. It was the fact that she had not been left destitute—far from it—that obviously puzzled reporters. Apparently Wally Flanagan had not understood the protocol for deserting husbands. It seemed clear that he intended to start over someplace else from square one.

"Not exactly," Phil Keegan said when they talked about the case during lulls in a Cubs game.

"Why do you say that?"

"He had a girlfriend."

"That's not in any of the stories."

"Cy found out about it, and he wasn't likely to feed it to a reporter. He ran into Flanagan and his popsy in a Loop bar."

"He actually met her?"

"It was the lead he pursued, but it led nowhere."

"So he must have learned her name."

Phil nodded, but he was distracted by the game.

"What was it?"

"Cy would remember."

"Sandra Bochenski," Cy said later, as if Father Dowling's question were the most natural in the world. But when had Lieutenant Horvath last shown surprise?

"And you tried to trace her."

"I was told she had relocated to San Diego."

"Who told you?"

"The doorman of the building in which she lived on the Gold Coast. She might have been just feeding him a story, but you never know. If that was the plan, he never got to California."

An eloquent Hungarian silence. They both seemed to be thinking of the mangled body that had been discovered in the cement mixer of one of the Flanagan trucks.

"But that was years after he disappeared."

Cy almost smiled, as if Father Dowling had hit on the important point. The real mystery lay there, in the years between the disappearance of Wally Flanagan and the discovery of his mangled body.

"Any idea what he did during that time?"

"It makes you think, doesn't it, Father?"

It did indeed. Nathaniel Hawthorne wrote a tale in which a man deserted his wife and lived for years just blocks away, undetected. Had Wally Flanagan spent those unaccounted-for years in Fox River?

Cy didn't think so. "Unless he became a recluse, he would have run the risk of discovery."

"It's too bad you can't pursue the matter."

Something in Cy's manner suggested that he had not lost all interest in these long-ago events.

"You were an altar boy here?" Phil Keegan had told Father Dowling of Cy's connection with the couple as pupils in the parish school.

"Not much of one."

"And Flanagan?"

Cy nodded, but that was all.

Tuttle was never thoroughly at his ease in Chicago, but then he found Fox River, where he was on the bottom rung of the legal ladder, intimidating. Nonetheless, the traffic, the buildings, the prosperity, the hustle and bustle of Chicago made him feel like a country bumpkin. He rode up the long escalator at Water Tower Place feeling little of the triumphant enthusiasm with which Hazel had dispatched him on this appointment.

"Mr. Tuttle?"

She rose from a little table in the atrium, a full head taller than Tuttle, and anyone except for the little lawyer from Fox River would have been rendered breathless by the mature beauty of the woman.

"I knew you by the tweed hat," she explained. "Your assistant told me."

Assistant? Was that how Hazel described herself? Perhaps he was lucky she didn't call him her assistant. He removed his tweed hat, put it on again, then took it off once more. He put out his hand, and she took it.

"Sandra Bochenski," she said.

He joined her at the table, a distracted waitress homed in on them, and they ordered coffee.

"I called you because you once worked for Melissa Flanagan."

Tuttle became wary. That long-ago occasion when his help had been enlisted to find Melissa Flanagan's lost husband represented one of the few peaks in his career. He had been of little help to her, of course, but no one else had any better luck finding Flanagan.

"That was a long time ago."

"I know." She looked around. "I wish this weren't so public a place."

It had been her choice, as far as Tuttle understood. Any place would have been more impressive than his office. "There's a little park across the street. With benches."

"Good. Let's finish our coffee and go there."

She went before him on the down escalator, equalizing their heights. They got safely across Michigan and soon were settled on a bench, with the old water tower conferring historical importance on the scene.

"I had an affair with Wally Flanagan," she said, looking him in the eye.

Tuttle tipped back his tweed hat to conceal his uneasiness. His knowledge of the shenanigans in which men and women got embroiled was largely theoretical. He never took divorce cases, in tribute to the long and faithful marriage his parents had known. What Sandra Bochenski had said would have provided a welcome lead when Mrs. Flanagan was his client.

"Tell me all about it," he managed to say.

She did. The little park was better than the coffee shop they had left, and Tuttle had the unsettling sense of occupying the role of confessor. She spoke with quiet intensity. She and Wally Flanagan had been in love, so they had decided to run away together and start a new life. He could make a fortune anywhere. She had gone ahead to San Diego and waited. "He never came."

Tuttle nodded, trying to convey some appreciation of the perfidy of males.

"I waited and waited."

"Didn't you try to contact him?"

"Where? I called his office, but I couldn't just ask. Weeks passed, and I began to realize that I had been jilted. I felt like a fool, of course."

"He wasn't here," Tuttle assured her. "I would have found him if he was."

She accepted the boast even though he had never discovered her affair with Flanagan. Was she telling the truth? It was not Tuttle's way to look a gift horse in the mouth, but her story made him uneasy.

She said, "His body was discovered here."

"That was years after he disappeared."

"I know! I want you to find out where he was during that time."

"What is your interest?"

"Of course you would want to know that."

"Any lawyer would."

"Who killed him?"

Tuttle thought of Peanuts, and his sense that this could be a dangerous client increased. "It could have been anyone."

"I think I know who it was."

Tuttle waited; his uneasiness increased.

"I would rather not mention his name now. That can come later. Will you undertake to find out where Wally was during those years between his disappearance and the finding of his body?"

"That is no small assignment."

"I can afford the expense."

His uneasiness lifted as memories of the fee he had earned from Melissa Flanagan came back to him. Sandra Bochenski's dress, her manner, and her bearing suggested that she could be a plentiful source of needed income. On any other occasion, he would have snapped at the opportunity, asked for a retainer, and sealed the bargain. Now he hesitated.

"You mustn't refuse me."

"Why me?"

"Because you already know more than any other lawyer could. You worked on the case."

"That's true." Her praise did not warm his heart. Superior knowledge in such a matter as this could put one in jeopardy.

"Well?" She had turned to look directly at him, and he felt at the same kind of disadvantage he always did with Hazel.

"Where are you living now?"

"In Chicago? The Whitehall."

"The hotel?"

"Yes." She paused. "I am thinking of moving back to Chicago. I'll be frank. This has become my mission. For years I felt that

Wally had made a fool of me. Now I don't know. I can only know if I learn what he did do when he left his wife. How he spent all those years until his body was found."

"Could there have been someone else?"

She glared at him and looked away. Her expression became tragic. "Of course, I thought of that."

"Is it possible?"

"You will have to find out." She turned back to him. "I find it hard to believe, I have to tell you that, but it does seem an obvious explanation, doesn't it? He was in a mood to run away, and if not with me, why not someone else?"

"His wife couldn't believe he would abandon her."

"I know. He always said she had no idea how unhappy he was with her."

"Why was he unhappy?"

"It will sound silly."

"Many explanations do."

"They had known one another forever, since they were children. His wife was beautiful, popular. Winning her was like a competition, and he won. He came to wish he had lost."

These were deep waters for Tuttle. He felt a residual loyalty to Melissa Flanagan. Romantic intrigue puzzled him. He might have been a Martian baffled by the way in which otherwise intelligent human beings make fools of themselves because of the flesh. Why couldn't all husbands and wives have the simple love and devotion his parents had had?

Sandra had opened her purse and taken out a checkbook, which she opened on the knee of one crossed leg. She looked inquiringly at him, and he knew he would not have the courage to tell Hazel he had refused the wealthy woman's offer.

"Do you have cash?"

"Only three hundred dollars."

"That will do."

"We could find an ATM where I could get more." She obviously did not object to keeping this on a cash basis.

"No, no. What you mentioned will do."

"And make you my lawyer?"

Getting married must be like this. She handed him three hundred-dollar bills. Benjamin Franklin seemed a stranger, and three images of him made him more so. Tuttle took off his hat and deposited the money in the band. She watched with a delighted smile.

"So that's the point of the tweed hat."

"You realize I am going to have to ask you a great many questions?"

"Should I come to your office?"

He thought of the crowded rooms on the third floor of a building whose elevator hadn't worked in years. "You say you're staying at the Whitehall?"

"We could have dinner there tonight."

"Let's say tomorrow night."

She took his hand in both of hers. "I can't tell you what a relief this is."

"I understand."

She stood, and he wondered if he should accompany her to the Whitehall, but again she took his hand in hers. "I really can't tell you how relieved I am. I feel I should have done this years ago. Until tomorrow? Let's say six thirty."

"Six thirty."

And off she went, suddenly just another well-dressed woman

in a crowd of people hurrying to hundreds of different destinations. He watched her out of sight and then remembered his car. The hourly rate of the garage in which he had left it was like the monthly payment he had made when he bought it. Tomorrow he would come by train to cut expenses. He took off his tweed hat, made sure Ben Franklin was comfortable, put it on again, and hurried off to repossess his car.

"I've retired," Luke Flanagan said, looking around Amos Cadbury's office almost with resentment.

"So I've heard."

"Biggest mistake I ever made."

"Then you've led a flawless life. Please sit down, Luke. You have to realize that my own duties have considerably diminished in recent years. I have become a remote presence to my juniors here."

"That's what I should have done. Die with my boots on."

Luke's shirt was open at the neck, no necktie, but that seemed to be the trend now, the wider world catching up with the wily entrepreneur's somewhat flamboyant sartorial style. Today he also wore a sport jacket of many colors and khaki pants. He sat across the desk from Amos, crossed his legs, not without difficulty, and widened his eyes. "Guess why I'm here."

Amos chuckled. "Last week a client your age sat there and told me he planned to remarry."

Luke didn't laugh. "You ever think of that?"

"If I ever do, I will reread 'The Miller's Tale.'"

"Don't know it."

"Is that why you've come?"

Luke hesitated. "My second biggest mistake was leaving my house in Fox River. Oh, I don't regret turning it over to Melissa, but where I live is full of transplanted old people. They call it a community, but what it is is a business. I should have invested in the place rather than moving in there. Old age is lonely enough without being surrounded by strangers."

Amos smiled receptively. Luke would get to the point of this visit in his own good time. Of course, the office must remind him of the long-ago time when he had drawn up the agreement with Wally after it was clear that his son had no intention of taking over the business Luke had built.

"Maybe if I had stood firm he'd be alive today, Amos."

"You can't know that."

"I know, I know." He shook his crew-cut head. "The worst part of being old and having nothing to do is that you sit around thinking, remembering, reliving the past. You listen to others only so you can talk yourself. That's why I stayed away from the parish center."

"At St. Hilary's."

"I didn't want to be *that* old. Melissa likes the place. At her age!"

"Many do."

Luke frowned. "I'm told that Gregory Packer is another habitué. More a son of a habitué as far as I'm concerned."

Amos remembered the man who had wept at Wally's funeral. No need to commend him for that to Luke. The old man had convinced himself that Packer was a bad influence on his son.

"Why I'm here, Amos, is this. I told you I spend a lot of time brooding. There are many things I don't understand, but right up there near the top is where the hell Wally was all those years before his body was found in one of my trucks."

Amos nodded. "That is a mystery."

"I want to solve it."

"To what purpose?"

"I just want to know. Where was he, what was he doing? Of course I thought he had run off with some woman. Maybe he had."

"Luke, even if he did, nothing would be changed by finding out."

"And then the way he died." Luke squeezed his eyes shut and turned away. "Did you ever see the inside of a cement mixer?"

"No."

A pause. "Did the client who sat here get married?"

"Not yet."

"Maybe that is the solution."

"What is the problem?"

"I told you. Loneliness."

Amos did not have to be told of the loneliness that follows on the loss of a spouse. Every day since his beloved wife had died, he had said a rosary for her. Often, alone at home, he spoke aloud to her, and at night vivid dreams of her still came.

"Do you have anyone in mind?"

"Maybe. Do you know what stops me? The fact that Wally probably did run away with some woman other than his wife."

"You don't know that."

"One of my daughters heard rumors."

It was unclear to Amos whether Luke was simply unburdening his soul or wanted legal assistance. Only someone who had been a client as long as Luke could have taken up his time like this. He decided to regard it simply as a visit from an old friend.

"How would I go about it, Amos?"

"Getting married?"

Luke's laugh was like a bark. "That I could handle. I meant finding out if Wally did take off with a woman."

"Did your daughter mention a name?"

Luke seemed relieved by the question. He took a slip of paper from his shirt pocket, unfolded it, and laid it on the desk.

Amos turned it so he could read it. "Had you ever heard of her?"

Luke shook his head. "Never."

"Nor have I."

"Don't worry about expenses."

It seemed a little late to tell Luke that Amos Cadbury was not the ideal person to hire for such a task. Then he thought of Phil Keegan. More to the point, he thought of Cy Horvath. There might be a way to get the information Luke wanted, although what he would do with it if he had it was difficult to say.

Luke got to his feet. "I'll let you know about the other thing."

Amos looked blankly at him.

"Getting married. "Another barking laugh, and then he thrust his hand at Amos. They shook vigorously. After the door closed behind Luke, Amos picked up the slip of paper. Sandra Bochenski.

11

When Father Dowling invited Edna Hospers and her husband, Earl, to have dinner with him at the rectory, Marie Murkin was dumbfounded.

"Dinner? Here?"

"Would you rather that I entertain them at a restaurant?"

"No!"

"Well, then."

Marie stood mute and stricken in the door of Father Dowling's study. None of the objections that doubtless surged in her breast could be voiced. Marie had always considered Edna a subordinate, doing at the parish center things for which Marie could not spare time from her rectory duties. This was not a view that Edna shared. She had been hired by Father Dowling; he had always expressed satisfaction with the way she had turned the empty school into a center where seniors in the parish could spend their days in company with one another. Marie's incursions into Edna's domain had often generated sparks, and once or twice Father Dowling had to negotiate the equivalent of the Treaty of Westphalia between them.

He felt that he owed the housekeeper some explanation. "It's a way to welcome Earl back."

"He came back months ago."

"So you blame me for the delay. I blame myself, Marie."

"I'm not blaming you at all."

"That's a relief. I know I can count on you to prepare something special."

Marie left, and a low keening sound followed her down the hall to her kitchen. It grew louder as the door swung back and forth and then closed behind her.

The point of the invitation was to convey to Earl something of the concern he had felt ever since Phil Keegan had linked the name Pianone to the discovery of Wally Flanagan's body in a cement mixer. Earl, on parole at last, had landed a job driving one of the Flanagan trucks. From Edna, Father Dowling had heard how pleased he was, and she, with the job. The news from Phil that the Pianones were seeking to invest in the company Luke Flanagan had built had turned the Pianone connection from a predictable rumor when a body was found in the locality to something less speculative and more upsetting. It would not do to have a man on parole working for a company infiltrated by a family like the Pianones.

He had thought of mentioning his concerns to Edna in the conviction that she would pass them on to Earl, but there were two things wrong with that. He had no idea what he might say to Edna, and there was no way of telling how whatever message he came up with would be passed on to Earl. The Solomonian decision seemed to be to tell them both at once, but rather than diminishing the difficulty, it doubled it. As the evening when the Hospers would dine at the rectory approached, Father Dowling feared that the occasion might easily go by without any mention of the dangers the Pianones might pose for Earl. It did not help that Marie was giving him the silent treatment. Unable to express with anything approaching charitableness, or even civility, how she felt about seeing her rival ensconced at the rectory dining room table, she locked her lips and threw away the key. Conversations with her had been reduced to nods and shakes of the head supplemented by a makeshift sign language.

"Cat got your tongue, Marie?"

Marie purred in reply, but the expression in her eyes was not benevolent.

"You've only set three places."

Marie made a face and stared at him.

"Of course you will join us."

"I have my own table in the kitchen."

"As you like."

He almost wished now that Marie would join them. The prospect of the dinner no longer looked inviting.

As it happened, it was Earl who brought up the Pianones. Rumors had floated around the yard at Flanagan's and among the drivers. "If they come in, I'm out of there."

"Oh, Earl," Edna said.

"I'd rather go back to repairing television sets than have anything to do with that bunch."

Mission accomplished without need for a word on his part. There seemed to be a lesson there. But then it was foolish to think that anyone could have more concern about himself than Earl. The sweet taste of freedom was still fresh for him, and he had no intention of jeopardizing it.

"Not that I think it will happen. The old man, Luke, really chewed out Frank Looney when he heard of it."

Marie came and went throughout the meal, more frequently than seemed necessary, her eyes cast down, her manner that of a menial. It did not help when Edna praised the food. Marie gave her a wintry smile and disappeared through the swinging door into the kitchen.

Marie was vulnerable to Earl's praise, though, and then he got up to examine the hinges on the swinging door. "I never saw any like these. You got a screwdriver, Marie?"

Marie found the tool, and Earl proceeded to tighten up the hinges. She asked him to take a look at the back door, too. "It's not a swinging door, of course, but it seems a little tilted."

They disappeared into the kitchen, and Edna looked at Father Dowling. "The house has never been as shipshape as it is since he got home."

Marie did sit when she brought Earl back, and she insisted that he have another serving of her pineapple upside-down cake. She beamed at his appetite. "Greg Packer was the same."

Earl stopped eating and stared at her. He put down his fork. "Why do you mention him?"

Too late, Marie seemed to recognize her mistake. Both Greg and Earl had spent time in Joliet. Edna, too, was quietly indignant. Marie retreated in confusion, and when she was gone, Edna told Earl, obviously for the first time, that Greg Packer spent time at the center. Whatever Earl's thoughts, he clearly had no intention of expressing them.

After the Hospers left, Marie again fell silent, but it was almost welcome now. It was as if she were giving herself the silent treatment.

They told Luke Flanagan that on the upper floors of the John Hancock you could feel the building sway. It must be like living on shipboard. His own apartment was on the top floor of the retirement community, and his windows faced the lake. It was better than television. He could sit there, looking out at the constantly altering surface of the lake, metallic gray, streaks of the brightest blue and all the shades in between, and the water just kept rolling in night and day. When he couldn't sleep, he would sit in the dark and enjoy the lights on the lake, reflections, some passing ship far out, sailboats bobbing in the marina, their masts doing what the Hancock Building was said to do. There was no sway in his building, but the lake offered constant proof of the influence of distant planets on the earth, the tides recording the pushes and pulls from outer space.

His apartment itself didn't interest him. There wasn't a stick of furniture from the house in Fox River, no photographs to invite grief or self-pity; he might have been living in a hotel. What else was the place? Temporary housing on the last leg of life's journey.

There had been one photograph of Dora, but he put it in a drawer after he started fritzing around with Maud.

"Maud what?"

She had a square face and what had once been red hair. "You won't laugh?"

"Try me."

"Lynn." She waited.

"I don't get it."

"Well, I won't explain it."

Until he did get it, Maud seemed some riddle he had to unravel. He began to spend a lot of time with her in the common recreation room he had hitherto avoided. She seemed genuinely interested in the concrete business.

"I supplied the cement that fireproofed McCormick Place."

"You did?"

"Remember the fire that nearly destroyed it?"

He liked her laughter. She liked beer. That got them out of their building and up the street to what Luke began to call their dive.

"Have you ever seen a Franciscan?" she asked.

"In here?"

"Our place is named after them."

"That's because you might just as well take the vow of poverty when you settle there."

"I don't think there are any Franciscans."

"Maybe it's because the place is for the birds. We used to have Franciscans in our parish in Fox River."

They never talked much about their families, but he had the sense that she was as disappointed in her offspring as he was in his. Just a long sigh and dismissive wave when she mentioned her three sons. One was in Alaska, another in Santiago, Chile; the third was a Trappist.

"A monk?

She nodded. "He went in right out of the army. If I see him once a year, I'm lucky."

"Where is he?"

"In Kentucky."

There wasn't much Luke could say to that. Parish priests were mysterious enough for him. He gave her the story of Wally in dribs and drabs. She was a good audience, but then her hearing wasn't much better than his. The slam and bang of cement mixers had deadened the nerves in both ears. He found hearing aids useless.

So had she. She stuck a finger in each ear and said, "Digital hearing aids."

She was fun. From time to time, there was a wedding in their community, a twilight union between two lonely people.

"What's the point?" Luke asked.

"I'll buy you a book."

"He's older than I am."

You couldn't watch a golf match on television anymore without being assailed by commercials for Viagra. That must be the explanation.

"Some people don't learn from their mistakes," she chirped. It seemed a rebuff.

"They'll save money, anyway. One apartment instead of two."

"And he gets a cook and housemaid."

"You cook?"

"Are you proposing?"

It began as a joke between them, but after a while Luke wasn't sure. Mentioning the possibility of remarriage to Amos Cadbury had been a preemptive strike. He wanted to hear a reaction to the possibility in the real world. Well, in Fox River. One day he drove Maud to Fox River and showed her Flanagan Concrete.

"You still own it?"

"My nephew Frank runs it."

He parked, and they watched one of the trucks emerge from the gate, the great mixer mounted on it turning slowly. Luke explained to her the process. "I started paving sidewalks and pouring the floors of residential garages. It grew from that."

"Your monument."

"Set in concrete."

Her husband had been a dentist. He had worn false teeth.

"These are mine," she said.

"So are these."

A gift horse? She laughed when he said it. She was fun to be with.

He had been alone the time he dropped in at the office and Frank told him he had been approached by one of the Pianones who wanted to invest in Flanagan Concrete. Frank seemed to find the offer attractive. "We could double the business."

"Frank, you do that and I'll can you and take it all back."

"It's just a business proposal, Luke."

"Sure it is. How long do you think you'd last if they got a foot in the door?"

Frank hadn't thought of that. He had a good head for cement but not much else. Unless he was thinking of returning to the Looney family's old habits. The fact that gambling was now legal and the Pianones had a lock on the local casinos made them seem legitimate. Luke drove immediately downtown and chewed out Robertson, the police chief.

When Luke mentioned the Pianones, Robertson grabbed his arm and pulled him into an inner office, shutting the door. "For God's sake, Luke, pipe down."

"If they try to muscle into my business, I'm holding you responsible."

Robertson went pale. Of course, he was chief of police only because the Pianones had put him there. The mayor was another Pianone puppet. Ye gods, what a town.

Luke went down a floor and talked with Cy Horvath, who listened to him with an unchanged expression. If you could choose sons, he would have picked Cy. Why the hell hadn't Wally been influenced by Cyril Horvath rather than Greg Packer?

Cy said, "If they're serious, they'll apply pressure."

"What kind of pressure?"

"You got any weak spots?"

After he said it, Cy fell silent. They were both thinking of Wally. Was that the meaning of the discovery of his body in a Flanagan cement mixer? The way Wally had died, along with the Pianone interest in Flanagan Concrete, suggested dark possibilities. Cy Horvath seemed to be having the same thoughts.

The real mystery was where the hell Wally had been during the years between his disappearance and the finding of his body. Luke had put Amos onto that.

Most of those staying at the Whitehall were out-of-towners, tourists intent on exploring the Magnificent Mile or Navy Pier, taking guided cruises on the Chicago River, and patronizing the city's restaurants and theaters. Not a few managed to get baseball tickets when either of the two Chicago teams was in town. The dress code in the Whitehall dining room was, given all this, informal, and Tuttle in his wrinkled seersucker suit stood out. The little lawyer had been tardy in his arrival, mumbling something about the interurban train he had ridden from Fox River. Now they were ensconced at a corner table, Tuttle on the banquette. Behind it was a huge mirror, but no multiplication of the man could have instilled the confidence Sandra Bochenski longed to feel in him. She reminded herself that this was the lawyer Melissa Flanagan had relied on to conduct a search for her husband.

"The trail has grown cold after all these years," Tuttle said when she asked if he had begun his investigation.

"He had to be somewhere!"

"Very likely far from here. Given all the publicity, anyone who recognized him would have informed the police."

Sandra thought of Ferret, the manager of the building in which she had lived before leaving for California. Surely Ferret would have recognized the man who was such a frequent visitor at her apartment if he had come upon a photograph in the newspaper.

"I've been thinking about what you told me. About the plan the two of you had to begin life anew in California."

"He never showed up."

Tuttle moved the bottle of beer he had ordered when the waiter took their order for drinks. "Let me tell you what the police would probably think."

"Have you told them?"

Tuttle shook his head. "You sure they don't already know about you and Flanagan?"

"How could they?"

"One of Flanagan's classmates is a police detective. Cy Horvath."

Just like that the memory came. She had met Wally in their favorite Loop bar, and there was a man with him, a man he later told her a bit about. He was a detective with the Fox River police. That had been months before she and Wally had decided to go off together, but she had sensed the disapproval in that hulking figure. The name could have been Horvath. Sandy was suddenly sure that was his name. Wally had also mentioned that Horvath, like half the men who knew her, had a crush on his wife. Surely a detective would have remembered that encounter when Mrs. Flanagan reported her husband missing.

"What would the police think?"

"That the two of you did meet in California. Years passed, and there was a falling-out . . ."

"I married another man."

Tuttle opened his notebook and waited, pencil poised.

"Gregory Packer. He may have had something to do with what happened to Wally."

"Why do you say that?"

"Because he seems to be courting Melissa Flanagan now."

Tuttle's hand went out to the tweed hat that was on the banquette beside him. She could see that the money she had given him was still inside. Would he put it on? He seemed to decide against this. He turned to a fresh page in his notebook. "I want to have as detailed a record as you can give me of your years in California."

She should have been prepared for this, but it unnerved her to have him scribbling away while she reconstructed her California years—San Diego first, meeting Greg, their marriage.

"What happened?"

"He hit me."

Tuttle frowned.

"I realized that all along he was after my money."

"What money is that?"

She told him about her portfolio and the way it had increased under Wally's tutelage. "It was to be our nest egg."

"Who knew of that?"

"No one."

"But you told your husband."

"I don't know how he could have, but I came to believe he already knew."

"How could he have found out?"

"I don't know. Have I mentioned that he had known Wally when they were kids?"

"He did?"

"They went to the same school."

"DePaul?"

"The same grade school, their parish school."

"St. Hilary's."

"Yes."

Tuttle sat back and looked at her. "You wanted to know what the police would think? You have to understand their mentality. They are going to wonder if maybe you and your husband didn't decide to get more money out of Wally Flanagan."

"He had disappeared!"

"They'll wonder if he really did."

"Oh, for heaven's sake."

This was no way to enjoy a meal. Eventually the waiter took away their scarcely touched entrées. Sandy asked for a manhattan.

"Another beer," Tuttle said to the waiter's inquiry.

They fell silent while they waited. When the drinks came, Tuttle looked at the bottle of beer and shook his head. "I could buy a six-pack for what that is costing you."

She smiled. "I can afford it."

"Good."

"Look, Mr. Tuttle, you are making your job seem to be investigating me. I am hiring you to find out where Wally was all those years."

"And you think your former husband knew?"

"I think he found out."

"And killed Wally?"

It was a terrible thing to accuse someone of, but yes, she did think that.

After a time, they withdrew to the lounge. Tuttle went over the chronicle he was constructing of her years in California: San Diego, then Oxnard, where she resumed her maiden name.

"He might have located you."

"I doubt that he even tried. He found someone else."

It seemed a useless exercise, but other memories came, filling in the chronology he was creating. None of it seemed to have the least importance, apart from her ill-considered marriage to Gregory Packer.

"Don't get me wrong," he cautioned her, "but I'll have to verify all this. It will be your protection if the police get interested."

She did not object, because guilt had been her companion from the time she and Wally had decided to go off together. He had assured her that he would leave his wife amply provided for, but that didn't lessen the awfulness of what they were doing. The ease with which he talked of leaving his wife had given her pause, as if she had some intimation that he would do the same to her. She had felt an odd closeness to his wife when she gave up waiting in San Diego, knowing Wally would not come to her. If he could betray his wife, he certainly could do the same to her. And he had. Of course, there were her investments, but then he had left his wife well provided for, too. How could she not wonder where he had gone, what he had been doing, during all those years before his body was found in one of his father's cement-mixing trucks?

"If I were you, I would begin with Gregory Packer," she said.

"I've already found out a thing or two about him."

"Oh."

"He spent three years in prison, right here in Illinois."

"He did!" It seemed best to pretend surprise.

She wanted all the details, and Tuttle gave them to her. Her sagging confidence in the little lawyer reversed itself. Maybe he would find out where Wally had been and what had happened to him at the last. Apparently he hadn't found out about Greg's marriage to the woman who owned the driving range. It was her all-too-convenient death that made Sandra sure Greg could have had something to do with Wally's horrible end.

Alone in her room, a thought she realized she had been avoiding formulated itself. What would it be like to sit down with Wally's wife and talk about what he had done to the two of them? She imagined them commiserating with one another. That was crazy, of course. How could Melissa Flanagan feel that their cases were at all similar? Besides, Melissa had renewed her old acquaintance with Greg Packer. Sandra sat perfectly still. Melissa ought to know what a monster Greg was.

Marie Murkin had mounted the steps to the back porch, grocery bags dangling from both hands, and was confronting the obstacle of the door when there was a clatter of steps behind her, a hand reached around her, and the door was opened.

"Madame!"

She looked up into the smiling face of Gregory Packer. "Have you been into the altar wine again?"

"Ho ho."

He followed her into the kitchen and helped her put the groceries on the table. She took off her hat, picked up the phone, pressed a button, and told Edna she was back. Father Dowling was on his monthly retreat, and Marie had asked Edna to monitor the rectory phone in her absence.

"No calls," Edna said.

"Thank you, dear." Marie turned to Greg. She tried to look stern but began to melt under the power of his boyish grin. For weeks, she had been resenting the fact that after his initial visit she had seen him only from afar, usually in the company of Melissa Flanagan. "And how are you getting on with the Widow Flanagan?"

He laughed in delight. "Is that what you call her?"

"That is what the other old ladies call her."

"Other than yourself."

He ducked when she took a playful swing at him.

While she put away the groceries, he sat at the table looking on benevolently. "Do you know what I like about being back? Nothing has changed. It's like a time warp. Here you are, doing what you've always done, peaceful and serene while all around you everything else is going to hell."

"Watch your tongue."

"I would need a mirror."

She could easily imagine him preening before a mirror. If anything was unchanged, it was his charming bad-boy manner.

"I suppose you want tea?"

"If you're out of altar wine."

She made tea the old-fashioned way, no bags, and soon the kettle was singing on the stove. Marie was trying to conceal her delight at this visit. It was all she could do not to tell Edna, when she had her on the phone, that Greg Packer had come to visit her. In his absence, she had come up with a long list of questions she wanted to ask him. When tea was ready and he had taken an experimental sip, then kissed his fingers with closed eyes, indicating approval, Marie began. "Where are you living?"

"I have a little apartment for the moment."

"Here in the parish?"

"It's above the garage at the Flanagan home."

"You're staying there!"

"It was an offer I couldn't refuse."

Marie looked closely at him. "What is going on between you two? You are the talk of the parish center, as I am sure you know."

"Mrs. Murkin, we were kids together."

"So were Cain and Abel."

He sat back. "What a comparison."

Much as she would have liked to pursue the subject, there were prior questions. "So you are out on parole."

He smiled sadly. "Is there anything you don't know?"

"About you I know nothing at all. Where have you been all these years?"

"Do you really want to know?"

"That is why I asked."

He finished his tea but put his hand over his cup when Marie lifted the pot. "One's my limit." He looked at her. "I think you do want to know. Okay."

He had joined the navy and never left land. He had stayed on in San Diego after his discharge.

"Doing what?"

"I golfed a lot. I ended up managing a driving range."

"You gave me the impression that you had married."

"Did I?"

"Did you?"

"Give you the impression?" A grin that soon faded. "Yes, I got married. A huge mistake that I eventually corrected."

"What does that mean?"

"It was only a civil ceremony." He paused so she could catch the significance of that. What kind of marriage could it have been if it hadn't taken place in church?

"You mean you divorced her?"

"Oh, it was mutual. No hard feelings."

"And then?"

"I went on managing the driving range. And played the field. Mrs. Murkin, my life has not been that of an altar boy."

"I should think not. And what about this parole?"

"Who told you about that? I thought nobody knew."

No need to tell him that her source was Cy Horvath. "Perhaps nobody does."

"Just you."

"If you think I am going to spread the news, relax. Tell me what happened."

Cy Horvath's account had the brevity of a police blotter. Stealing from the till when he tended bar in the Loop. In Greg's account, it was largely a misunderstanding. "If I'd had a decent lawyer, I would have walked."

"And this happened in Chicago?"

"I should have stayed in California."

"So what are your plans?"

"That's what I want to talk to you about."

This was more like it. Marie hitched her chair closer to the table. She was on her second cup of tea and in a pastoral mood. Thank God Father Dowling was away for the day and she had full scope for her ministrations.

"It's unfair, but because of my misfortune getting a decent job is difficult."

"Of course."

"I have a dream. What I would like to do is start my own driving range. It's something I know. I have found two places, either one of which would be perfect." He looked beseechingly at her. "But I need a little capital."

Father Dowling did not golf, although most priests did. The Franciscans had been fanatics. That did not commend the sport to Marie, but she had the idea that golf was a wholesome occupation—out in the fresh air, exercise, far from the temptations of the world.

"How much?"

He sat back. "Marie, I am not asking you for money."

"That's a good thing. I am poor as a church mouse." Not wholly true, but she did not want to encourage any hopes in the direction of her savings. "But maybe I can help you find someone."

"Marie, you do that and I'll give up altar wine."

"We'll see. Now, about the Widow Flanagan."

He pushed away from the table. "Fear not, madame. You have my heart."

He snatched her hand and kissed it before she could pull it free. Then he was in the doorway, his hand on his heart. "Mrs. Murkin, you are the best."

"Oh, call me Marie, for heaven's sake."

"Farewell, Marie for heaven's sake."

And he was gone, the door closing as he clattered down the steps. From the window, she watched him go off in the direction of the school, but abruptly he stopped. He looked toward the church and then directed his feet toward the side door. He disappeared into the church, and Marie realized her eyes were misty. The lost sheep had returned.

The great question was how to approach Amos Cadbury about setting Greg Packer up in business. Go through Father Dowling? Of course, that was the best way, but would he be sympathetic to the idea? She remembered her faux pas when the Hospers came to dinner. Mentioning Greg Packer had obviously been a big mistake. She hadn't dared bring it up with Edna since that night.

Cy Horvath's response when Amos Cadbury asked him if he could provide information that would enable him to determine what Wallace Flanagan had been doing and where he was during the years between his disappearance and the discovery of his body in a cement mixer would not have encouraged someone unacquainted with the phlegmatic lieutenant. The slightest of nods, no promises, but Amos was certain Horvath would be of help.

"How will you begin?" Amos asked him.

"He might have gone to California," Cy said.

"Why do you think that?"

"He was mixed up with a woman in Chicago before he deserted his wife."

"Sandra Bochenski."

"How did you know that?"

"How did you?"

"Years ago, I ran into them in a Loop bar when I was in town to check up on some things. He introduced her as a client, but it was pretty clear what was going on."

"Did you follow that lead at the time of the disappearance?"

"I went to where she had lived and found that she had gone off to California."

"With Wallace Flanagan?"

"I suppose that was the plan."

"Were they traced?"

"Mr. Cadbury, it was not a high-priority case. Missing persons seldom are. We were swamped with other things, and besides, Mrs. Flanagan had hired someone to track him down."

"Tuttle!"

"I know. But dog will have its day."

"Not Tuttle."

"I may not be able to do much better."

Amos permitted himself to doubt that, however cold any trail would have grown after all these years. Three days later, Cy was back with a printout showing a marriage in San Diego.

Amos was puzzled when he read it. "Sandra Bochenski?"

"The one Wally was carrying on with in Chicago."

"But the groom. Gregory Packer. Isn't that . . ."

Cy nodded. "It's possible that Wally would have used his old friend's name. Once he and the woman were concealed behind an assumed name, it would be less likely they could be traced."

"This is the man who was at Wallace's funeral?"

"Who is now living in the apartment over the garage at the Flanagan home."

Amos threw himself back in his chair. "What would Luke Flanagan say to that?"

In subsequent days, Cy informed Amos that the San Diego marriage had apparently been dissolved. The woman, using her maiden name, had lived in Oxnard, where she seemed to have prospered. That was how he had been able to trace her, checking out Sandra Bochenski.

"And the man?"

Cy handed over photocopies of the travails of Gregory Packer, accused by his employer, a woman, of trying to take over the business and her assets.

"A driving range."

"A driving range."

"She brought charges?"

"And subsequently dropped them. She married him."

"Another marriage!"

Cy had one more photocopy, a story of the death by drowning of Cecilia Packer, found in the family pool by her husband.

Amos remembered how moved he had been when Gregory Packer wept at the funeral of his boyhood friend Wallace Flanagan. Cy gave Amos an oral report of the mishap that had landed Packer in Joliet.

"That's about it so far."

"But nothing on Wallace Flanagan?"

Cy shook his head.

*　*　*

Amos believed that nothing that happens, however apparently obscure and unimportant, escapes the omniscience of God. History consists of the more or less unrelated deeds of billions of free agents, the collective meaning of which eludes human understanding. A Toynbee, a Gibbon, a Spengler could write accounts that suggested an intelligible significance to all those billions of human acts, but such accounts were made possible only by ignoring the vast majority of things that went on in the world. Historians concentrate on historically important figures, meaning those agents who caused most trouble for others, launching wars, new orders, world conquests, but the innumerable foot soldiers in their ventures were swallowed up in the prideful ambitions of the leaders. Surely their importance was not exhausted by being a footnote to the ambitions of an Alexander, a Napoleon, a Stalin, or a Hitler. Only God knew that.

Cy's report suggested some modification of this view. Now satellites hung above the earth, their cameras recording what went on below. Computers were filled with data no human memory could contain. The pervasive presence of government, something Amos deplored, had created bureaucracies and records that mimicked divine omniscience. Now Amos had a number of facts, more than he could have imagined possible, but he lacked any means of interpreting what they meant. Out of the past Cy had pulled the record of two marriages and of the charge against Gregory Packer of seeking to bilk his employer, a problem that had been solved by one of those weddings. Then the woman had drowned. Presumably Gregory Packer had then come into possession of the wealth he had coveted.

Using contacts of his own, he made inquiries about the driving range outside Ventura, California. It had been claimed by eminent domain, giving way to a shopping center. It was then, apparently, that Gregory Packer had migrated back to the Midwest, tending bar in the Loop. It seemed a humble occupation for a man who had come into some money. Perhaps he had no special skills—but why work at all? It had been a fateful choice, leading to indictment and conviction. Now he was on parole, a frequent presence at the parish center at St. Hilary's and occupying the apartment over the garage at the house Luke Flanagan had built for his family and lately turned over to his daughter-in-law, Melissa. Surely Melissa had no knowledge of the checkered background of her childhood classmate. Amos felt a professional as well as personal obligation to warn her, but how?

Hazel could say what she liked about Peanuts, Tuttle knew better, and now he had further proof of the value of his friendship with the Pianone contribution to the Fox River police.

"Cy's working on that," Peanuts mumbled, his mouth full of egg roll.

Tuttle was surprised that Peanuts had been listening. One of the features of their friendship was that Tuttle could ramble on about his practice, what, if anything, he was working on, without any fear that what he had said would be passed on. By and large, it wasn't even heard, but Peanuts had perked up when Tuttle mentioned his new client.

"Working on what?"

"The woman you mentioned."

"Sandra Bochenski?"

Peanuts's interest in the matter was exhausted, though, and he attacked a massive dish of shrimp fried rice. Tuttle was rattled. However mixed his reaction was to acquiring his classy new client, the news that Cy Horvath was interested in Sandra Bochenski was unsettling. Clients like this were, not to put too fine a point upon it, rare in Tuttle's practice. Yet she had called him; Hazel had set up the interview.

"How'd it go?" Hazel asked when he returned from the Loop.

Tuttle plucked one of the Bennies from his hat, carefully concealing the other two, and dropped it on her desk. "We have a client."

"What's she like?"

Tuttle decided against an accurate description of the woman who could have been a model in her youth and was still a most attractive female. Hazel, in the manner of her gender, had a limited appreciation for accounts of the attractions of other women. "Well preserved."

"How old?"

"Middle-aged."

Hazel picked up the bill and put it in her account book. "You should have asked for more."

"She offered more."

"And you turned her down?"

"Strategy."

Hazel laughed a derisive laugh, and Tuttle went into his inner office, sailed his hat at the coatrack, and then scrambled to pick up the two hundred-dollar bills that fluttered to the floor.

"What are those?" Hazel demanded from the doorway.

Tuttle handed over one. She held out her hand for the other, but he jammed it into his shirt pocket. "Expenses."

Hazel let it go. "Keep accurate records."

Alone, he retrieved his hat and settled into the chair behind his desk, put his feet up, and pulled his hat over his eyes, trying to think of how he could fulfill the assignment he had taken on.

He had thought of Horvath but vetoed the idea. Why should the police do his work for him? They had their chance years ago. So had he, of course, but Melissa Flanagan had accepted his failure to find her husband with good grace. That was when the thought of having a chat with his old client occurred to him. Now Peanuts's alarming suggestion that he and Horvath were on the same trail again brought the thought that talking with Melissa could do no harm and might do some good. Besides, it would salve his conscience. Accepting as a client the woman who by her own admission had been Wally Flanagan's lover seemed disloyal. He had always liked Melissa.

He drove to the Flanagan house in his own car, Peanuts being unavailable for chauffeur service. Tuttle had been told that Officer Pianone had called in sick. Peanuts kept accurate track of his sick days, lest he fail to claim one. Tuttle might have gone by the Great Wall to see if his friend was soothing his imaginary illness with sweet and sour pork, but having made up his mind to talk to Melissa, he did not want to delay.

Concordia, the avenue on which the Flanagan house stood,

was lined with dwellings several notches above the usual in St. Hilary's parish, but the Flanagan place added notches to those. It was a monument to Luke Flanagan's success, and he had called in favors from various associates in the building trades to make it everything a self-made man could want. Here he had raised his two daughters, both now gone to fat and living far off, and Wally, the heir apparent who had turned away from the role awaiting him. Owner of Flanagan Concrete? What must it be like for a father to hear his son express contempt for the business that had put food on the family's table, built the house in which they lived, and given his children advantages he himself had never had? Not many fathers would have set up Wally the way Luke had. Tuttle, who had come through adversity to something short of success, compared his devotion to his own father to Wally's callous treatment of his. So what was the lesson, avoid success? Now Luke was living in Chicago, Wally was dead, the daughters were putting on weight elsewhere, and Melissa occupied the family house.

Tuttle turned into the long drive and inched toward the house, leaning over the wheel to get a good look at it. Everything seemed in perfect repair; the shrubbery was trimmed; the lawn might have just been mowed. The driveway branched off, and Tuttle had the choice of going under the porte cochere at the front of the house or on to the four-bay garage. There was a middle-aged man shooting buckets at an old basket mounted above the garage doors. He went on shooting when Tuttle parked, and not even the unoiled complaint of the driver's door disturbed his concentration.

"Damn!" he shouted. He had just missed a shot. He turned to Tuttle. "Nineteen in a row."

"Did I throw you off?"

"Yesterday I hit twenty-three."

He was a tall drink of water with an air of easy familiarity that gave Tuttle confidence. Was the man an employee? Perhaps he was the groundskeeper, but the pale blue slacks and silk shirt told against that. His highly polished loafers gleamed. Without warning he passed the ball to Tuttle. The little lawyer caught it with a wild movement of his arms, bringing it against his chest as if it were a baby.

"Take a shot."

Tuttle returned the ball. "I haven't shot a basket since I was a kid."

"Neither had I. It all comes back. What can I do for you?"

"Tuttle." He thrust out his hand.

"Packer."

The scales dropped from Tuttle's eyes. Gregory Packer. This was the man his client thought might have had something to do with the death of Wally Flanagan, and there he stood with a disarming grin, youthful good looks, and the air of the lord of the manor.

"I saw you at the funeral."

"The funeral?"

"Wally's." He added, "A long time ago."

Packer peered at him. "You a friend of Wally's?"

"Well, I know his wife. She was a client of mine some years ago."

"A client."

There were one or two calling cards in Tuttle's tweed hat, but there seemed no need to waste one here. "I'm a lawyer."

Tuttle was dying to know what Gregory Packer was doing

hanging around the Flanagan house, shooting buckets as if he owned the place.

"If you came to see Melissa, you're out of luck. She's having lunch with her father-in-law."

Tuttle's wonderment must have been written on his face. He had removed his tweed hat and rubbed his face with his free hand.

"You're wondering what I'm doing here."

"That's none of my business."

Packer pointed. Tuttle thought his gaze was being directed to the backboard, and then above it he saw windows.

"My apartment. Melissa was kind enough to let me have it while I get settled."

"No kidding."

"You should see the place."

"I'd like to."

He had surprised Packer, but then the man seemed delighted. "Come on, I'll show you."

Behind the garage, an outside stairway rose to the entrance to the apartment. Packer let them in, switching on a light. It was cool, obviously air-conditioned. They were in a very large living room off which a bedroom opened on one side and a kitchen on the other. A television with a huge screen was on, its sound muted.

"Pretty nice."

"I haven't lived this well in years."

Knowing that in the man's past there was a marriage to Sandra Bochenski, one that had ended in divorce, Tuttle wondered if Packer's ease and comfort had not gone into steep decline when he came home to find that his wife had skedaddled with the money he had hoped to get control of.

When they went outside again, Packer asked Tuttle to stick around and shoot some buckets. "I keep the ball a little soft, so you get the benefit on rim shots."

"I wish I had the time."

If Melissa was having lunch with her father-in-law in the Loop, there was no point in waiting for her. As a concession to Packer, he took the ball and heaved it toward the backboard. Swish. Nothing but net. Packer cheered. It was all Tuttle could do to go on to his car and get out of there. He had never made a bucket like that before. But character prevailed. He wanted to get downtown and find out if Cy Horvath was checking out Gregory Packer as well as Sandra. The trail to one would surely lead to the other.

Ferret, the manager of the building where Sandra Bochenski had lived, just looked at Cy. "I know you."

"We talked years ago."

Ferret was still thinking.

"About a woman who used to live here. Sandra Bochenski. I wondered if you had seen her lately."

Ferret stepped back, his mouth twitching, putting his little mustache in motion. "That *was* years ago. She went to California."

"I understand she's back."

"No kidding!" His delight was short-lived. "Well, she's not back here."

"It was just a thought."

"Geez, I wish she was. What a fine woman."

Well, it had been a long shot. Cy left. His car was in a lot on Michigan. It had been a long walk from there to the building, as if he were punishing himself for going on a wild goose chase. Going back, he thought of stopping somewhere for a beer, but that brought memories of the time he had run into Wally and the woman Sandra had joined them and Cy had just known his old friend was fooling around. Being a cop means being mixed up with the seamy side of life, but when the people involved were friends, those you have known since you were a kid, it was different.

Ever since Wally had vamoosed, Cy had been certain there was a connection with the woman he had met with Wally in the Loop bar, but missing persons did not fall within the scope of the department run by Phil Keegan. Even if they did, Cy figured Wally was just another husband who had run off with another woman, however incredible it seemed that he would leave someone like Melissa. He had talked with her and not discouraged her wild hope that Wally was afflicted with amnesia and wandering around somewhere wondering who he was. His efforts to turn up Sandra in San Diego had been perfunctory. For one thing, he wasn't sure he would be doing Melissa a favor by discovering her husband shacked up in San Diego. For another, they were suddenly swamped with cases that did concern the department. A body was found in the Fox River with a rope around the ankle, apparently loosened from the concrete block that had been meant to make it fish food. It was the body of a foot soldier in the diminished ranks of the Looneys, a family that had finally lost out to the Pianones in Fox River. The poor slob had been given a magnificent funeral, with Looneys and Pianones shedding crocodile tears. They had been poised on the brink of a war, but then the Looneys threw in the sponge. One of the Looney boys joined the Jesuits, and the heir apparent, Frank, a nephew of Luke Flanagan, took the place in the business the old man had hoped Wally would fill.

When Wally's body was found in the cement mixer, Phil Keegan's first thought was that the war between the Looneys and Pianones had only been postponed, but that had made no sense. The Looneys no longer represented a threat; the old man was dead, one son was a Jesuit, and the other was running Flanagan Concrete, where the body had been found. Only a cop with a long memory would recall that old rivalry. The Pianones in the meanwhile had become almost respectable. Once their major interest, gambling, became legal, they launched a fleet of moored craft where gamblers could throw away their money, and their sleazy bars were sold or made respectable, all the women hanging around in them amateurs, products of the sexual revolution. Why should a man pay for what he could have for the price of a couple of drinks and listening to some woman gripe about her husband?

The obvious explanation of Wally's death was no longer applicable, but that made it more mysterious rather than less. Now, belatedly, at Amos Cadbury's request and with Phil Keegan's blessing, Cy was finally trying to piece together the lost years of Wally Flanagan. All he had come up with was the lost years of Sandra Bochenski.

The wedding in San Diego between Sandra Bochenski and

Gregory Packer was a surprise until Cy wondered if Wally had used their old friend's name to throw off anyone who might be trying to locate the couple. The subsequent stories about Greg Packer and the owner of the driving range he managed, ending in marriage, made it unlikely that the accused was Wally. Indeed, newspaper photographs made it clear that the culprit was Gregory Packer. That woman, Cecilia, had been found drowned in her pool. It was declared accidental, but how could Cy not wonder if Greg Packer had decided to become sole owner of the driving range? So what had happened to Sandra Bochenski? A helpful colleague had scanned databases and come up with a Sandra Bochenski in Oxnard. Cy had been ready to fly out to interview her but received word that she had returned to Chicago. Hence the trip to her old apartment building in the wild hope that she might be there.

Cy was on Michigan when a couple emerged from the little park around the old water tower. The tweed hat in this kind of weather would have caught his attention in any case, but there was little doubt that it was Tuttle. The woman, Cy would have bet his pension on it, was Sandra Bochenski. Cy watched them, keeping out of sight. They parted, Tuttle heading in one direction, the woman in the other.

Cy followed her to the Whitehall Hotel. He waited several minutes and then went in. "Is Sandra Bochenski staying here?"

A blank look. Cy read the clerk's name tag and asked the question again in Hungarian.

The broad face lit up. He punched the computer and said, in English, "Eight-oh-three."

Cy wrote it down.

"You can use the house phone." He said this in Hungarian.

"How long has she been registered?"

The clerk became wary, and Cy showed him his identification. All camaraderie was suddenly gone. Who knows what memories were awakened in the transplanted Hungarian? He suggested that Cy talk to the manager.

Cy took a chair in the diminutive lobby and thought. Now that he had located the woman, he wasn't sure that he wanted to confront her until he knew why she had been talking with Tuttle. That suggested that she would be around for a while. If he did call her room and she came down, she might clam up like the clerk, and there wasn't much he could do about that. He decided that having a little talk with Tuttle first was the way to go.

"Get him out of there."

"Dad!"

Luke Flanagan paused and rubbed his face, as if to remove the scowl brought on when Melissa told him she had let Gregory Packer use the apartment over the garage. He had always been proud that she was his daughter-in-law, and her calling him Dad moved him.

"He was a friend of Wally's, you know that."

"A bad influence. The guy's a bad apple, he always was."

"It's only temporary."

"How long is that?"

"I didn't set a deadline."

"Then I will. I don't want him staying there."

"I'll take care of it. I didn't think you'd mind. What's the point of an empty apartment?"

Luke had turned the huge attic over the garage into an apartment for himself when he had imagined Wally and his wife living in the house. One more plan gone to hell. He had convinced himself that Greg Packer was behind his son's decision to refuse to take over the family business. Hearing that the man was now settled in the apartment over the garage was like a kick in the stomach.

He and Melissa were in the cafeteria of the retirement home where Luke lived. He looked around at the old people scattered among the tables, and the scowl returned. What the hell was he doing in a place like this? It had seemed a good decision: Plunk down a wad of money and say good-bye to all the usual frets and cares of living; no more bills, only the phone bill; he had house-keeping service, a neighborhood with dozens of distractions. But how many times can you walk along Navy Pier and find it interesting? Several times, Luke had come back to his building semi-drunk from sitting over a series of beers, half watching a game on television, bored stiff.

"What's he do, anyway?"

Melissa smiled. "He shoots baskets."

Luke stared at her. He had put up that backboard himself, and he had memories of playing one-on-one with Wally. Losing to his son had never hurt although he hated to lose at anything. Wally's winning was like himself winning, so how could he lose?

"I want him out of there."

"Okay. Okay."

Luke looked at her. Melissa was still beautiful, and she had held her chin up during the long period while the search for Wally went on and afterward. His daughters thought she would marry again, but she hadn't. If she had, it would have been like the final blow to his hopes. Suddenly Luke understood why he reacted so strongly to the news that Greg Packer was occupying the garage apartment. He was Melissa's age; they had known one another as kids; proximity was a dangerous thing between a man and a woman—and of course Melissa was a woman. The character that had kept her loyal to Wally could be worked on by a bum like Packer. The thought of the man moving from the garage into the house was too much. "I mean it."

"I said all right."

"I'll go back with you."

"No, no, Dad. I said I'd take care of it. I really had no idea you would object."

"So why did you want to see me?" he said, his tone turning a page in the conversation.

"Do I need a special reason?"

Her hand covered his. She still wore her wedding ring. God bless her. Luke still wore his, all these years after Dora was gone. He turned his hand and squeezed Melissa's. "More coffee?

She shook her head.

"I don't blame you. It's weak as dishwater."

"Have you made lots of friends?" She was looking around the cafeteria.

"The place is full of widows."

"Be careful."

"Ha." Thank God Maud wasn't in evidence. There was no way he could avoid introducing Melissa to her.

The thought seemed fanfare for her appearance. In the lobby, the elevator doors opened, and Maud stepped out, saw Luke, and came right up to him. She looked at Melissa with mock suspicion. "Is he trying to pick you up?"

"Maud, this is my daughter-in-law!"

Thus Maud was introduced to Melissa, and Luke could only imagine what stories would begin to circulate. Ever since he had hinted to Amos Cadbury at the possibility of remarrying, he had regretted it. Melissa was beaming at Maud. Her arm went around Luke. She might have been blessing them.

"Maud is one of the cleaning ladies."

"Oh, stop it, or I'll scrub out your mouth."

They went on, he and Maud, like a comic routine, to Melissa's delight. Damn it.

"Beautiful girl," Maud said when Melissa had kissed him, patted Maud's arm, and gone through the revolving doors.

"Girl! She's middle-aged."

"And you said your daughters were fat."

Luke let it go. Now that Melissa was gone, his anger that Gregory Packer was occupyng the apartment over the garage in the Flanagan house in Fox River returned. If Maud hadn't shown up, he would have driven to Fox River and kicked that SOB out of the apartment.

"I'll buy you a beer."

"Only if I can buy you one."

"That sounds fair."

She took his arm and steered him toward the revolving doors.

It was good to have her back from visiting her son the monk in

Kentucky. She told him about the guesthouse where the monks put up visitors, just across the road from the monastery, and gave them retreats.

"Some stay in the guesthouse longer. Thinking about joining, I guess. One of them was your namesake."

"Luke?"

"Flanagan."

"No relative of mine would think of becoming a monk."

"What else are you?"

Her eyebrows danced, and she pressed her knee against his beneath the table.

"A retreat didn't do you much good."

"I'm better at advances."

"You can say that again."

"Another beer?"

"They make me amorous."

"Good." She signaled to the waitress.

Tuttle sauntered into Cy Horvath's office, took a chair across the desk from him, and tipped back his hat. "Why don't we pool resources?"

Cy just looked at him.

"The Wally Flanagan case. I've been hired to find out what

he was doing from the time he left here until he turned up dead."

"Is that what Sandra Bochenski wants to know?"

Tuttle sat back. "How do you know that?"

"You've been under surveillance."

"And you've been checking out Sandra Bochenski." Two can play at that game.

"What else did Peanuts tell you?"

"So you see, we have a common interest."

"I thought you were interested in Wally Flanagan."

"Let me tell you what I've learned."

Tuttle took off his tweed hat and fitted it to the knee of his crossed leg. While he spoke, he had the impression that none of what he had to say came as news to Cy, but with that face you never knew. He told Cy about the affair between Sandra and Wally and about their plan to run away together and start a new life in California. "She went ahead. He never showed up."

"Is that what she told you?"

"Are you saying he did?"

"You're doing the talking."

"You realize that I am under no obligation to tell you these things. It's all confidential. But why should we duplicate efforts?"

"You could just have Peanuts get you my report."

"I'd rather hear it from you."

"How long is Sandra Bochenski in town?"

"Until I find out what she wants to know."

"What's her interest?"

Tuttle had thought about this. Why should his client be paying him good money to find out things that could not do her any good. Curiosity? That seemed the only motivation. Of course, she was still a woman scorned, but any revenge she had in mind involved Greg Packer, not Wally Flanagan. Her suspicions about Packer seemed Tuttle's hole card.

"What's your interest?" Tuttle asked boldly.

"I'm a cop."

"Things must be pretty slow around here if you can devote your time to ancient history."

"You think Wally Flanagan is ancient history? How long has it been since his body was found?"

"Long enough to be forgotten."

Even as Cy said it, Tuttle considered what that meant. The body of Wally Flanagan had been mainly hamburger. The identification had been made by his wife from the wedding ring on the undamaged left hand. A ring can be put on any dead hand.

"Get the hell out of here, Tuttle. I've got work to do."

Tuttle rose. "I just had an idea."

"I thought I heard a buzzing sound."

"More like ringing."

He found Peanuts napping in the pressroom and shook him awake. "Can you get a car?"

"What's wrong with yours?"

"I'm low on gas."

Peanuts rose slowly. "Meet me downstairs."

Tuttle took the circular staircase that gave those going up and down a view of the dome above and the great checkerboard floor of black and white tile below. What if the death of Wally Flanagan had been staged? He had to ask Melissa what had happened to the wedding ring that convinced her the body in the cement mixer was her husband's.

He waited outside, and five minutes later Peanuts drove up with a patrol car.

"Couldn't you get an unmarked car?"

"Look at the dents in the fenders."

You never knew with Peanuts. Tuttle got into the passenger seat, and Peanuts took off, turning on the siren briefly, then grinning at Tuttle.

"Leave it on."

"I don't want to get arrested."

After she left her father-in-law, Melissa drove to St. Hilary's. She smiled as she thought of the perky little woman with whom Luke had been so friendly. Was it possible that he would marry again at his age? It seemed a comic possibility, but that wasn't fair. His life had been as devastated as her own by Wally's disappearance. In his case, it went back further, to Wally's turning down the offer to succeed his father in the family business. That had opened the way for his cousin Frank.

"Frank Looney?"

Wally had nodded. The famous, or infamous, Looney family.

"But that's all over. My cousin Jim is a Jesuit, and Frank is straight as an arrow."

When she parked, she looked toward the school, wondering if Greg was there. How the years fell away when she was with him; they might have been kids at school again, in that very building. He was full of memories of those days. The past, if you got far enough back in it, was like a soothing shower.

"Of course, we were all nuts about you."

"Oh, sure. Why didn't you marry?"

"I did."

"Tell me."

He looked at her, then shook his head. "It's not a happy story."

"It can't be as sad as mine."

"In a different way."

"Are you retired or what?"

"Oh, I have a business plan. All I need is money."

He told her about the driving range he'd had in California, and his tone told her how much he had enjoyed it.

"So why did you leave?"

"The state decided to run a freeway through it."

"Then you must have made money."

"Oh, I did. Then I remembered how Wally made his money, with money, and tried my hand at that. I might just as well have run it all through a shredder."

Money had never been a problem with Wally, and he had left her amply provided for. When he went missing, people kept coming back to that since it suggested his disappearance was part of a plan. Only in the most private compartment of her soul could she admit that thought. Her great fear during the investigation was that information about Wally's fooling around with other women would be turned up. When she had hired Tuttle, she had been aware of his reputation. Amos Cadbury's reaction told her exactly what he thought of his fellow lawyer. The truth was that she had never expected Wally to be found. They had gone together forever by the time they married, and they were too used to one another. She had watched him grow bored with her, but then she was a little bored with him, too, not that she would ever have been unfaithful. Men are so different. The thought that he had deserted her made weeping easy when she was questioned about him.

As the years passed, their life together seemed almost as unreal as his disappearance. She found that she didn't mind living alone. Her only regret was that they had never had children. God knows they had tried. Maybe that was the reason he had begun to stray. Left well provided for, she had sought diversion in cruises, in travel. She would arrive in a city like Rome ready for systematic touring, having read up on it for months before leaving. But how much diversion can one stand? There was the consolation of religion, of course, and she had become in her way devout. How ironic to remember that Wally had told her that when they were in St. Hilary's school and he an altar boy, he had dreamt of becoming a priest.

When his body was found and she was shown the ring she had put on his finger on their wedding day, it seemed proof that for years he had been living his life, ignoring her, not caring at all about the pain his disappearance caused her. She had looked at it with tear-filled eyes but could only shake her head when the ring was offered her. It seemed to mock her life and the grief she had sincerely felt when she could convince herself that something awful had happened to him or that he had amnesia and just didn't know who he was. If Amos Cadbury had been shocked by her refusal to take the ring, he managed not to show it.

She sat now in her car, staring at the school she and Wally and Greg had attended, and Cyril Horvath, too. Whenever Cyril had talked with her, she had the sense that he knew far more about her and Wally than he let on. Some old people were moving slowly around on what used to be the playground. Luke thought she was crazy, spending so much time there. Well, it was crazy. You would think she couldn't wait to be old.

Of course, it was being with Greg that explained it. It wasn't being old, it was being a school kid again.

"All I need is money," he had said about his plans to open a driving range. "I found a perfect spot, out in Barrington."

"How much money?"

He told her, just a guess. It didn't sound like much to her. People who saw them together would think what she had thought when she saw Luke with Maud. Was that what she wanted? She realized it wasn't. How stupid to let him use the garage apartment. Luke's anger seemed to indicate that he thought there was something going on between her and Greg. Well, there wasn't, and there couldn't be. Getting that money for him would be the easiest way to put an end to it without having to confront him.

Melissa got out of her car and went rapidly along the walk to the rectory. Mrs. Murkin came to the door in response to her knock. The housekeeper looked surprised, then delighted, but finally settled for a bland, wide-eyed waiting look.

"Is Father in?"

He was. Mrs. Murkin showed Melissa to a front parlor and

marched off down the hallway. There was a delightful aroma of pipe smoke in the house, competing with the smell of baking. Then Father Dowling was with her, tall, thin, regarding her with the most kindly eyes.

Father Dowling had heard the story first from Edna, just an aside as she was bringing him up to date on the center, then from Marie, who spoke with a stiff and staring look that made it clear she thought he had to do something about this. Phil Keegan had also passed on what he had heard from Cy. Gregory Packer was living at the Flanagan home. Only Marie had put it quite that baldly, adding, "With Melissa Flanagan." She had adopted a kind of chant tone for this recital, and "Flanagan" came out in a flutter of neums. Phil just sounded disgusted when he told the story.

"It must be a very large house," Father Dowling said. A pastor has wide responsibilities, but he did not know that his writ ran to this sort of thing.

"Oh, he's not in the house. There's an apartment over the garage."

"Marie will be relieved to hear that."

He said this on the assumption that Marie Murkin was keeping her ears open as she pushed a dust mop around in the hallway outside Father Dowling's study.

"What does Cy think of these arrangements?"

Phil half rose and pushed the door shut. "We've learned quite a bit about Packer in recent weeks."

Father Dowling had already been told that Greg had spent time in Joliet and was now on parole, but that was recent history. It seemed that Greg had remained in California after getting out of the navy.

"And he married."

Father Dowling waited. Half the people in the world were married to the other half.

"The woman that Wally Flanagan had been having an affair with."

"He married her!"

Phil seemed pleased with all the information on Packer Cy had managed to gather.

"Had he known her before?"

"He was in the navy. She was in Chicago."

That Packer should meet and marry the woman who had gone to San Diego in the expectation that Wallace Flanagan would join her there invited speculation.

"Of course, we thought Flanagan might have used Packer's name. They went to school here, you know."

"Did Wally Flanagan go to California?"

"If he did, he left no trail. With the woman, Sandra Bochenski, there was the wedding record. Packer was even easier. After the marriage broke up . . ."

"Is there a record of that, too?"

"Packer divorced her, charging desertion. That was when he married the woman whose driving range he was managing."

"A busy fellow."

"A bad apple." Phil said this with the quiet conviction of one who had been dealing with Gregory Packers all his life. The idea that people might change was only an abstract possibility for him, given his years of experience. Father Dowling's own experience taught much the same lesson, which is why what most of us need is mercy rather than justice. Now Packer was a frequent presence in the parish center and had moved into the garage apartment at the Flanagans'.

Marie's attitude toward the former altar boy had changed radically. Her account of his dropping into her kitchen out of the blue had been almost breathless, and for a time she had just tossed her head at the mention of his name, but as of late she seemed quite enamored of the man all over again. "He's Edna's responsibility, not mine."

"I thought you were in charge of altar boys," Father Dowling had commented.

"Hmph."

Altar boys were a thing of the past now. Father Dowling found that he preferred saying Mass without one, not that there were all that many boys in the parish anymore. Nor did he enlist the aid of eucharistic ministers, who swarmed over the sanctuary in most parishes, their help unnecessary and making the distribution of Communion a protracted and distracting process.

"Maybe you ought to talk to Melissa,"

"Doesn't she know about his checkered past?"

"She's a woman." Phil seemed to think that covered a multitude of weaknesses. Well, he had a lot of poets with him on that score. Frailty, thy name is woman. Father Dowling made no promises, not that Phil expected one.

Now Melissa had come to the rectory. "I want you to say a Mass for Wally. My husband."

"Of course."

She opened her purse, and he put up a staying hand. "No need for that."

"But I would like you to say more than one."

"How many?"

She looked at him sadly. "Of course, you know the story. What on earth was he doing all those years after he left me?"

"The police are looking into that now."

"They are?" She seemed undecided whether to feel good about it. "After all these years?"

"Well, the finding of your husband's body brought it to their attention again."

"But that, too, is years ago."

Uncertain if he should tell her that it was at Amos Cadbury's urging that the investigation had been undertaken until its completion, Father Dowling remained quiet, allowing Melissa to reflect on his silence.

"Sometimes I think I don't want to find out."

"I can understand that." How much did she know? He had no inclination to tell her that the woman her husband had planned to run off with had married his boyhood friend Gregory Packer, who was now living in the apartment over her garage.

She turned and looked out the window. "I think I've done something stupid."

He waited.

She faced him again. "You know Greg Packer."

He nodded.

"I've let him use an apartment over the garage, and my father-in-law is furious."

"And you think it was stupid to do that."

"I should have thought of what it would look like to others."

"Gossip?"

"It's silly, of course, but suddenly it struck me how others might interpret it."

"I assume it's temporary."

"But I didn't say for how long. He's trying to get settled."

"It probably would be wiser if he settled somewhere else. Than in the apartment, I mean."

"To me, he's just a little boy I used to know. Most of the time, we talk about what we did as kids."

She seemed to want him to say something, but he didn't know what that might be. "So how many Masses would you like said?"

"Once a month?"

The Mass book was there in the parlor. He opened it and began to write. This time when she opened her purse, he did not stop her. Marie would never forgive him if he did.

"I suppose it's all confidential," Marie said when Mrs. Flanagan had gone.

"Not all."

Marie perked up.

"You've made a conquest."

Marie was puzzled. "But I haven't spoken two words to her."

"I meant Gregory Packer."

Marie stepped back, biting her lip, then fled down the hall.

* * *

A call from Amos Cadbury the following day told Father Dowling how Melissa had decided to solve her problem. "She wants to lend him the money to open a driving range."

"Ah."

"You've heard about the episode in California."

"Are you afraid she might marry him?"

"Good Lord. Don't even think it. Luke would hit the ceiling."

"What advice did you give her?"

"She's a grown woman, Father. If she wants to waste money on that fellow, there is little I can do to stop her."

As it turned out, Amos would be involved in the transfer of money. "I want to make sure he uses it for the purpose for which it is given. I've asked him to come see me."

Gregory Packer did not show up for the appointment. Amos, not used to being stood up, had his driver take him to the Flanagan house, going around to the garage. He mounted the steps to the apartment and was surprised to find the door unlocked. He pushed it open. The late Gregory Packer lay on the floor in a dried pool of blood.

Part Two

1

Cy, having been informed directly by Amos, picked up Dr. Pippen in the coroner's office and set off for the Flanagan house.

"What's so hush-hush?"

"I want to take a look before sounding the alarm."

Pippen shrugged. Then she was distracted by the neighborhood. "Such lovely houses! What happened?"

"Progress."

"Some of them seem in pretty good repair."

But not all. Many a young family who took on one of the grand old houses in this part of Fox River was surprised by what it cost to maintain such a place.

"Is this your old neighborhood, Cy?"

"Where I grew up is now a freeway."

"More progress?"

"Believe me, the house was no loss."

Nonetheless, he wished it were still there so he could at least drive by and look at the house he had grown up in. Greg Packer's house, a duplex, had gone to eminent domain as well. Of the three old friends, altar boys at St. Hilary's, only Wally had a house that still stood, and he hadn't given a damn.

Amos Cadbury's driver had backed the lawyer's car down the driveway, effectively blocking it. He was standing beside the rear door, on the lookout, and when Cy drove up, he tapped at the window. Amos emerged slowly from the backseat and waited for Cy and Pippen to come to him. The venerable lawyer bowed to Pippen and then looked wordlessly at Cy. He nodded toward the garage.

"Will you need me, Lieutenant?"

"You're not leaving?"

"Oh, no." Still, it was obvious that Amos would have liked to flee the horror he had come upon.

Cy swung up the driveway with Pippen at his side, a bag slung over her shoulder, her ponytail swishing. Only God knew how delighted Cy was by their proximity.

The door to the covered stairway was open, but before going up, Cy looked around. He was beginning to wish that he had treated this as an ordinary case, but the anguish in Amos Cadbury's voice had prompted this unusual procedure. Pippen, too, was looking around. She said to Cy, "See anything?"

He shook his head and started up the stairs.

Amos had left the door of the apartment open, too, and again Cy looked about before going inside. He went around the body, and then Pippen was kneeling beside Gregory Packer.

"Dead?"

"As a mackerel."

While Pippen called for the medical examiner's team, Cy walked slowly through the apartment.

The living room looked as if it had been tidied up, and the kitchen was unusually spick and span for an aging bachelor's. No dishes in the sink. The place mats on the table seemed to protect the wicker basket that served as a centerpiece; it was empty. It seemed unlikely that Greg Packer had been such a fastidious housekeeper. Cy eased open a cupboard. Stacks of dishes and cups. Neat as a pin. This place would have to be dusted for fingerprints. Then he noticed the rubber gloves draped over the edge of the sink. Even so. Only a professional would leave no fingerprints at all.

Pippen was back on her cell phone, wondering where in the world the truck with her crew was. They were on their way. Cy called the police lab to get their crew out here as well. Then he stood and looked down at the dead body of his old classmate. The moment called for prayer. He pulled out his phone and called the St. Hilary rectory.

Father Dowling got there before either of the crews. He knelt beside the body, eyes closed, a ribbonlike stole over his shoulders. His lips moved, and he made the sign of the cross over the remains of Gregory Packer.

"He's already dead, Father," Pippen said.

He nodded, but his expression suggested that at the moment he was open to theories that death comes on long after the so-called vital signs are absent.

Pippen's crew then arrived, and Cy went with Father Dowling to Amos Cadbury's car, which had now been backed into the street to admit official vehicles. The lawyer looked at the priest.

Father Dowling nodded. "I gave him conditional absolution."

"Rest his soul."

Cy cleared his throat. "Tell me all about it, Mr. Cadbury."

2

The violent death of Greg Packer brought a stunned stillness to St. Hilary's parish.

In the senior center, men and women who had been more or less ignored by Packer when he was with them, preferring to be alone with Melissa Flanagan, now remembered him with affection, even grief. Memories that over long lifetimes had learned the art of selection brought back a Greg Packer who had been one of them. He had never played bridge or shuffleboard, he had not played billiards, and few could have recalled anything he had said to them or vice versa, but when the news came, it seemed a call for mourning.

"We should all go over to church and recite the rosary for him," Mimi Popich said.

Lenore Holland let out a little cry. She was still holding her cards, fanned against her bosom lest anyone see what she held.

Gino Bacci suggested a moment of silence.

"Good. Good idea."

Chins dropped to chests. Lenore took another peek at her cards before closing her eyes.

"May he rest in peace,"

"Amen."

"Who wants to go over to the church?" Mimi asked, but she was ignored.

They would have to keep a collective eye on Mimi. Bursts of showy devotion were often danger signs. Advanced age could make people think they could offset a lifetime of humdrum attention to religious duties with a razzle-dazzle ending. Spending hours kneeling in the church or at the grotto or sighing aloud could be the beginning. Mimi herself had taken to wearing a shawl over her head and shoulders when she stopped by the grotto or went to church, affecting a peasant look as if she were trying to be Saint Bernadette. Usually these enthusiasms burned themselves out like a fever, and the old man or woman was no worse for wear, maybe even better for it, but there was always the possibility that a bout of exaggerated devotion would give way to a compensatory skepticism.

Gino Bacci, who had done well with his pizza parlor until Domino's moved into the neighborhood, had been saying fifteen decades of the rosary every day, for the late Mrs. Bacci but for himself as well. That might have been all right, but then he started making Holy Hours in the church. It was when he asked Father Dowling if the church could be left unlocked at night so he could get in that it was clear he needed to be brought down to earth. They hid his beads; they went with him to the church and carried on conversations in the pew behind him. Finally a more desperate remedy was needed. Lenore Holland was called into action. "But I knew Maria," she protested.

"All the better."

Lenore stuck to Gino like glue, hanging on his arm, babbling away about how much she missed Maria. He tried to get away, but she had a good grip on his arm, and then she was whispering into Gino's copious ear. They wandered up the path to a bench. For three days, they were inseparable. When he became a pest, Lenore told him to go peddle his papers.

"I sold pizza."

"Do you play cards?"

"No. But I can learn."

"Come back when you have."

That cast Gino for the role of village atheist, and he began to make remarks to shock the ladies. They just made faces at him, but Tim Toohy protested. "We have to answer for every word we say. You better be careful."

"You think God's listening?"

"Of course he is."

"All over the world, to everybody?"

"It's a mystery."

"You can say that again."

"It's a mystery." Of Tim, Gino was wont to say that he was not a fastball pitcher.

But Gino, too, was hit hard by the news of the death of Greg Packer, hence his proposal of a minute's silence for their fallen friend. Friend? Well, you know what I mean.

"I never know what you mean," Tim said.

"Show me how to play bridge."

Like many of limited intelligence, Tim Toohy was a masterful card player. He picked up a deck, riffled it, cut it, shuffled, did everything but run the cards up his arm. A friendship was born. Gino would have liked to show Tim how he had sailed a disc of dough toward the ceiling, caught it, twirled it, flipped it up again. Art speaks to art.

"I suppose there was a falling-out," Tim said.

"What do you mean?"

"With the Flanagan woman. He had moved in with her."

"Come on."

"An apartment over the garage. The one old Luke had meant to live in."

"You knew Luke?"

"I worked for the SOB." Tim had shocked himself.

"You were in cement?"

Tim had been a dispatcher, sending out the trucks. The two men stared across the table at one another. The phrase had brought back the fate of Luke Flanagan's only son.

"You know what I thought when they removed the body from the mixer?"

"I don't want to hear." Gino was damned if he was going to let Tim get started on the Pianones.

"Packer's death is probably connected with that."

"You watch too much TV. Deal the cards."

The fact was that Gino had seriously thought of enlisting the help of the Pianones when the competition from Domino's affected his business. He did talk to Marco, the Pianone who collected his insurance. Marco listened, nodding, saying nothing. The next day he was back. "Sell."

"I have been in this location for thirty years."

"It's time you had a rest."

Gino sold. The poor devil who bought the place thought he was getting a thriving pizza parlor when Gino, fearing the deal would fall through, told him, "They only deliver," which was true at the time but unlikely to stay that way, and within a year the buyer had declared bankruptcy. In and out of business so quickly the Pianones hadn't even bothered to offer him any of their protection.

As soon as Edna Hospers heard, she telephoned Melissa. The phone rang and rang, unanswered. She phoned the rectory and told Marie Murkin the news.

"God in heaven," cried the housekeeper.

"I tried to reach Melissa."

"Did you try her father?"

"I don't know him."

"I'll take care of it."

Edna hung up and sat at her desk. She was filled with foreboding. Ever since the remark about the Pianone interest in the firm, Edna had felt uneasy about Earl working there.

Earl had dismissed the possibility that the Pianones might move in on Flanagan Concrete. "Frank's a Looney. That's his name. His family used to be in competition with the Pianones, but they got smart and became legitimate. One of the sons is a priest. Frank Looney isn't going to let those people muscle in on him."

That he might not want it was one thing, but how did you resist the Pianones if they made up their mind to do something? Sweet reason was not the preferred method of persuasion with the Pianones. She tried to feel reassured by Earl; after all, if anyone should worry about his associations, it was him, but she felt a lingering unease.

"Busy?"

Edna looked up at the smiling face of Gino Bacci. Ever since she had caught him in a classroom with Lenore Holland, he had been dropping in on her unannounced. The business with Lenore was over, whatever it had been, and Gino had developed a bad habit of wanting to talk about religion. His recurrent topic was marriage. "We always said it was for keeps, right?"

"That's right."

"Why? Because of the kids. Mom and Dad stayed together to raise the kids. That was the idea."

"What's wrong with that?"

His smile widened, as if she had just made a bad move in checkers. "Once they're raised and out of the nest, what's left of the argument?"

This was puzzling. Gino had been a devoted family man; he was now a widower. His argument seemed to have no personal point to it. Or did it?

"Lenore is a widow," Edna said.

The smile disappeared. "What's that got to do with it?"

Edna dipped her head and looked at him. No need to mention how she had found the two of them together.

He got it. "Kid stuff."

He had not been thrown off his stroke for long. There was a second part to his argument. People of a certain age, a man and a woman, well, they're not going to have any children. So why can't they just pair off as they please? What's the difference?

"Who do you have in mind?"

"Are you married?"

"Get out of here."

He went laughing to the door, and Edna followed him to make sure he left. He was harmless, and he got a kick out of talking. Maybe his late wife hadn't given him much of a chance.

Before she got the door closed, he pushed it and looked back in. "I came up here to talk about Gregory Packer."

"Mr. Bacci . . ."

"Gino."

"Gino. You've caught me at a bad time."

He had pushed his way into the office again. He shut the door behind him. When he spoke, it was in a whisper. "I can't tell them this myself." He leaned closer. "Tell them the Pianones. They'll understand. And don't mention my name."

"What possible connection is there between Greg Packer and that family?"

"Just tell them, okay?"

And he was gone.

As soon as Tuttle heard of the murder of Greg Packer, he telephoned the Whitehall to speak to his client, but Sandra Bochenski did not answer when his call was transferred to her room. Maybe just as well. Tuttle folded his cell phone and looked across the table at Peanuts Pianone. It was Peanuts who had offhandedly mentioned the body in the garage apartment at the Flanagan home in Fox River. Tuttle's first reaction had been one of relief to think that this would free him from his ambiguous clients, but it quickly gave way to anxiety at the thought of losing his most profitable assignment.

"How would you like to drive me to the Loop?"

Peanuts looked at him from his narrow eyes.

"You on duty?"

The sound that escaped from Peanuts might have been a chuckle.

"We could have a beer on Navy Pier."

The path to Peanuts's consent was through his belly. At the moment it was chock-full of sweet and sour pork, three egg rolls, and a pot of hot tea, but the drive to the Loop would restore his appetite.

The car in the lot of the Great Wall was a patrol car, and that enabled Peanuts to zigzag down the interstate at seventy as if they were in pursuit of Public Enemy Number One.

"Take it easy," Tuttle cried when Peanuts nearly took the front fender off a car as he cut in front of it.

Peanuts answered by turning on the flashing lights and siren.

Geez. Tuttle pulled his tweed hat over his face after checking his seat belt. He kept forgetting that Peanuts behind a steering wheel had the mentality of a teenager.

When they got off the Stevenson, Tuttle gave Peanuts instructions to the Whitehall.

"I know where it is." He meant Navy Pier.

"I have to run an errand first."

"After we have a beer."

"No! Come on, Peanuts, I'm buying." Tuttle had picked up the tab at the Great Wall, too. Even so, Peanuts was pouting when he pulled to the curb in front of the Whitehall.

Uniformed porters converged on them and then, seeing the markings on the car, stopped, puzzled. Tuttle hopped out and pushed past them into the hotel.

The little lobby was crammed with baggage, and at a desk the concierge was doing a brisk business selling baseball tickets, excursions, and theater seats to clients who thought they were getting a bargain.

"Sandra Bochenski," Tuttle said, elbowing aside a Japanese couple at the registration desk. "Official business," he added.

He had to spell the name for the clerk, who fiddled with a computer keyboard and then frowned and fiddled some more. She looked at Tuttle. "She checked out."

"Checked out? When?"

"Today."

"What time today?"

"Early this morning." The clerk lost interest, and the Japanese elbowed past Tuttle.

He turned away. Maybe his client had changed her mind and headed back to California. Without telling him? He got out his cell phone and called his office.

"I've been trying to reach you," Hazel scolded.

"Any messages?"

A snort. "Lieutenant Horvath called."

"What's the message?"

"He wants to talk with you. I told him to try the Great Wall."

"Did Sandra Bochenski call?"

Hazel's attitude toward his client was mixed. On the one hand, hard cash had been put into Tuttle's hand, with the prospect of much more. On the other, Sandra was a woman, and Hazel was that most formidable of foes, a male chauvinist in skirts. She seemed to think there was something vaguely illicit in a woman hiring a man. Of course, Tuttle had not leveled with Hazel as to why Sandra had hired him.

"Why would she call?"

"Then she didn't?"

"No."

"I think she left town."

"Where should I send the bill?"

"I'll let you know."

He turned off his cell phone before returning it to his pocket.

Outside, taxis were lined up for half a block behind the patrol car, unable to pull in for passengers. Behind the wheel, Peanuts stared indifferently ahead, ignoring the frantic pleas of the porters.

Tuttle hopped in. "Let's go."

Peanuts took off with a squeal of tires, and in five minutes they were at Navy Pier, where Peanuts pulled into a convenient handicapped space and shut off the motor. He looked at the Ferris wheel, the people, the excursion boats, and the flags and pennants flying everywhere and grunted approval.

Tuttle had two beers. Peanuts was on his fourth when the little lawyer pulled out his cell phone and called Cy Horvath.

Cy wanted Tuttle to make Sandra Bochenski available for questioning.

"You've got to be kidding. About what?"

"She might help us in an investigation."

"The death of Greg Packer?"

"Have you already talked to her about that?"

"She left town. Checked out of her hotel in the Loop. Vamoosed."

Silence on the line, and then, "At your suggestion?"

"I'll forget you said that."

"I can always repeat it."

"The answer is no. I went to the hotel to talk with her and found she had left."

"Where are you now?"

"In the Loop."

"Have Peanuts get you back here fast, Tuttle. Or would you prefer that I ask Hazel about your client?"

"Within the hour."

"Drive carefully."

Whatever instrument had been used to strike and kill Greg Packer was nowhere to be found in or near the garage apartment.

"Something heavy," Pippen said when Cy asked her what it might have been.

"That helps."

"You want guesses?" She tossed her ponytail and looked saucily at Cy. In some possible universe, he would have taken her in his arms and told her he loved her. In the actual one, he simply nodded.

"That's right."

She rattled off a list: It could have been an ashtray, it could have been a candlestick, it could have been a chair, it could have been a croquet mallet . . .

"They're all accounted for."

"All what?"

"Croquet mallets. In the garage."

So something heavy had been used to smash the base of Greg's skull. The blow did not suggest a professional job, but then a professional would know that.

Before he called Tuttle, Cy wanted to account for the where-abouts of Melissa Flanagan, just to be thorough. It was really Luke he was thinking of, the irate father figure who had blown up when he learned that his daughter-in-law had let Greg Packer move into the garage apartment. Of course, it wasn't just the apartment that explained Luke's reaction. He had long ago cast Greg in the role of the friend who had misled his son. Turning away from the family business had been symptomatic, and leaving his wife might have seemed just a continuation of irresponsibility.

When he called Luke's condo in Chicago, a woman answered.

Cy hesitated, then said, "Mrs. Flanagan?"

She laughed. "That'll be the day. This is Maud Lynn." Pause. "A friend."

"Is Luke there?"

"Would I be in his apartment if he weren't? Who is this?"

"Lieutenant Horvath of the Fox River police. Let me talk to Luke."

"He's in the shower. The old fool decided to take up jogging and came back half dead. I had to help him upstairs."

"Tell him I called."

"Any message?"

Cy hesitated. The woman was obviously a chatterbox. "No, just tell him I called."

By the time Luke called back, he would have learned about the death of Greg Packer.

Cy would have liked to ask Pippen if she'd like a cup of coffee, or maybe a beer across the street. Just to talk, he told himself. Instead he talked to himself. It was absurd to think that what had happened to Greg was somehow connected with the renewed interest in finding out where Wally Flanagan had been during the years after his disappearance, but the thought came nonetheless. Greg had married Sandra Bochenski, who had gone off to California to wait until Wally joined her. It strained credulity to think that Greg had just happened to meet Sandra, who had been fooling around with his old friend Wally.

Cy shook his head. He had been trained by Phil Keegan, and the cardinal rule of any investigation was not to dream up some story of what might have happened. Stick to what you know. Okay, so what did he know?

Greg Packer was dead, killed by a blow to the head in the garage apartment of the Flanagan home.

Melissa and Greg had been an item at the St. Hilary parish center. Cy himself had seen them together and reacted somewhat as he had years ago when Sandra Bochenski came into the Loop bar to meet Wally. Melissa had offered the garage apartment to Greg and discussed with Amos Cadbury the possibility of financing his plan to open a driving range in Barrington.

Luke, who had never liked Greg, had been furious when he found out that Melissa had let Greg live in the garage apartment.

Sandra Bochenski, like Greg, had reappeared in Fox River years after Wally's body was found in a Flanagan cement mixer.

Inevitably, the manner of Wally's dying suggested the Pianones, but then the Pianones came to mind whenever there was a gruesome murder. Not that any Pianone had ever been indicted or convicted of murder.

So where to begin? At the beginning, more or less. What had become of Wally's old brokerage firm?

Brenda Kelly sat behind the counter that divided the reception area at Kruikshank and Sharp Investments from the financial gambling that went on behind her over phones and computers. Her head just cleared the counter, and she felt like John the Baptist after the dance, her body invisible to people coming in, as she answered the phone and dealt with the walk-ins. Some clients liked to just come in and sit, watching the parade of numbers that represented their security. The only rule of investing Brenda had learned when she worked for Wallace Flanagan was buy low and hang on. Buying and selling daily was for the big boys. The market itself took care of the small investor, lifting his boat with all the others. Brenda herself put her money exclusively into mutual funds and tax-free municipals. That was her advice to investors, which explained why she had ended up as a high-level receptionist. Kruikshank and Sharp liked lots of daily transactions, which spelled prosperity for the firm if not always for its clients.

"It was Mr. Flanagan's rule," she had replied when her conservative approach was criticized by Mr. Sharp.

Sharp's forehead wrinkled. This was the ship Wally Flanagan had deserted to go into business for himself. After his disappearance, K&S inherited his clients, and Brenda as well. "You're not working for Flanagan now," Sharp said. He had a perpetual smile, but it did not radiate any cheer. Maybe he had gas on his tummy.

By mutual agreement, she had been put at the reception desk. Among other things, she accepted checks that people brought in to add to their account and gave them a receipt, ignoring the phone while she was helping them. Her own smile, she was certain, radiated cheer.

It was a boring job, she had no illusions about that, but she was single, without much of a family since her parents passed away, and like the clients of K&S her thoughts were on a nebulous future when she would retire and enjoy the fruits of her cautious investments. Florida? She hated Florida. Just somewhere sunny without a lot of bugs. Sometimes she thought she was thinking of heaven rather than retirement.

Sylvia Beach, her closest friend at Flanagan's, had not made the move to K&S, and that made Brenda the expert on the disappearance of her old boss. Not that she knew much more than anyone else, but over lunch with the other girls she could make a few facts go a long way.

"It had to be another woman."

Brenda smiled enigmatically.

"But his wife is beautiful!"

"What has beauty ever done for me?" asked Laura, presumably a joke. Laura's teeth rested on her lower lips; she wore huge out-of-style glasses and piled her hair in a kind of pyramid atop her narrow head.

Brenda wondered what Sylvia would have said if she had been in on such conversations. Of course, that had been when Brenda first came to K&S, when the disappearance of Wally Flanagan was a hot topic. Time passed, and Wally was forgotten, which was maybe what he had wanted when he went away. Sylvia had been devastated. There had been something between Wally Flanagan and Sylvia, something that went beyond his restless generic interest in every presentable woman in the office. But Sylvia had decided to leave Flanagan Investments before K&S took it over. Like Wally, she seemed just to disappear.

The afternoon Lieutenant Horvath came in the door, looked around, and then advanced on the reception desk, Brenda knew immediately who he was. The years hadn't changed him much.

"Do you remember me?" he asked.

"Officer Horvath."

"Lieutenant."

Brenda gave him a salute.

"You worked with Wally Flanagan."

"That's right."

"Where can we talk?"

"We're talking."

Horvath looked beyond her at the busy advisors, most with headsets so they could talk with clients and operate the computer at the same time. "Can you take a break?"

Brenda took a break and led him down a hallway to the lunchroom. She realized that she had been expecting another such visit since the discovery of Wally's body. She drew a cup of coffee for him and hot water for herself. When they sat, she began to dip a tea bag in the water and waited.

"This is where Wally Flanagan got his start, isn't it?"

"That's right."

"You've heard about him, haven't you?"

"I was at the funeral."

"Strange case. When he disappeared, there weren't many leads, and we didn't follow up on all those we had."

"Oh."

"What was that other girl's name?"

Girl? Well, she and Sylvia had been girls back then. "And I thought you were interested in me."

"I'm a married man." His expression didn't change. "But then Wally was a married man, too."

She nodded.

"Sylvia Beach," he said. He must have remembered her name all along. "There was some indication of something going on between her and Wally."

"Who told you that?"

"You, for one."

"I did not!"

"Not in so many words, but the suggestion was there."

"Wallace Flanagan was a very friendly man."

"Does the name Sandra Bochenski mean anything to you?"

Brenda sipped her tea. Lukewarm. She would put a complaining note in the suggestion box. "No."

"Wally was having an affair with her. They planned to run away to California."

"No!"

"Sandra Bochenski?" He looked at her to see if the name rang a bell now.

"Why wasn't that made known at the time?"

"We didn't know it then."

"What difference does it make now?"

He explained it to her. Wally Flanagan disappeared, and then years later his body was found in a cement mixer at his father's place of business. A dead body is of more interest than someone's disappearance. "There are a lot of unaccounted-for years, and they could explain how he ended up in a cement mixer."

Brenda shuddered. She wished he would stop mentioning that. She'd rather think of Wally as he had been when she worked for him, a vibrant, good-looking man, even if he had preferred Sylvia to her. Frankly, the whole thing sounded pointless to Brenda. What good would it do if the police found out where Wally Flanagan had been between the time he disappeared and the discovery of his body, or parts of it, in a cement mixer?

"I was looking over the record of the interviews we did with you back then . . ."

"They were recorded!"

"These are the notes we turn in while we're working on a case. Did you know cops always end their day writing reports?"

"And you keep them all?"

"They're all on the computer now."

"That's spooky."

Horvath neither agreed nor disagreed, but Brenda felt that he liked the thought of those records no more than she did.

"So you don't know Sandra Bochenski. Is Sylvia Beach working here, too?"

"Why do you ask questions you already know the answers to?"

"To see if the answers you give are true."

"No, Sylvia Beach does not work here. She didn't make the move when K&S took over Flanagan Investments. In fact, she quit before the move was made."

"What was going on between her and Wally?"

"I have no idea."

"Good girl. Let me tell you a little secret. Wally and I were kids together, same school, same class, same neighborhood almost. His wife was also in our class. This is more than professional curiosity for me."

She believed him. Not that the tone of his voice changed, or his expression. Maybe he always told the truth. It was clear to Brenda that when he spoke of Melissa Flanagan, something important from when he was a kid was involved. It was a strange thought, that a police investigation could have such personal meaning. Then it occurred to Brenda that she had a personal stake as well. She had worked for Wally Flanagan; she knew his wife, who had dropped by the office infrequently and insisted on being introduced to everybody. The trouble was that this happened each time, and she didn't remember those she had already met. Cy Horvath asked her again if she had ever heard of Sandra Bochenski.

"There was something between her and Wally?"

"She thought they were running off to California together."

"Maybe I did hear about her. Not by name, but Sylvia was worried. I don't know what she expected, from a guy like Wally. Did she think he was going to leave his wife, his business, everything?"

"Do you know where she is now?"

"Sylvia? No."

After he left, Brenda went back to her desk, checked out a few sites on the computer, and then, just for the fun of it, checked the list of K&S clients. There it was, Sylvia Beach. The address given was in northern Minnesota, Garrison, wherever that was. There was a phone number, too. Brenda dialed it, and far off in northern Minnesota a phone rang—but then there was a squeal and a recorded message. *This number has been disconnected.* Hmm.

When she reviewed Sylvia's account, she learned that there had been fairly frequent transactions years ago, but then the account seemed to grow inactive. It continued to earn, of course. The question was, where were the quarterly reports sent? There was an e-mail alternative to snail mail. Brenda tapped out a message. *Sheila! Greetings from Kruikshank and Sharpe. How long has it been? Drop me a line. Brenda K.* But she felt as though she was the one dropping a line into unknown waters.

"Come on along, Boleslaw," Luke said. "Maud and I are going for a beer."

"Is it okay?" Boleslaw seemed to think that he was confined to the building. Not that he could get very far by himself in his wheelchair.

"Of course it's okay," Maud said, getting behind the chair and wheeling it toward the doors.

Bringing Boleslaw along was Luke's buffer against having to talk with Maud about yesterday when he had stumbled into the building. The sight of Maud made him want to blurt the whole thing out, but he wouldn't have made much sense if he had.

"Jogging!" she had cried, and it was like a punch line. She helped him to the elevator and into his room and told him to get into the shower.

"I'm not that kind of date."

"Can you undress by yourself?"

"Shame on you."

She pushed him into the bathroom and closed the door. He got out of his clothes, holding them up to the light to see if there were any signs of what he had just been through in Fox River. Under the shower, he let the water pound against him, keeping his eyes open so he could control his memories. He thought he heard a phone ringing, but then he always heard phones ringing when he was in the shower.

Now Maud wheeled Boleslaw up the street to their dive, maneuvering him through the oncoming flow of pedestrians. The door of the bar was narrow, and Luke had to get in front and lift the chair to get it inside. Bolelaw's eyes lit up at the sight of the bar, the illumined signs, the array of bottles on shelves behind it. Maud moved a chair and wheeled him up to a table and asked what he wanted.

"A boilermaker."

"Sounds good."

It did sound good. Luke ordered one, too, but Maud stuck with just beer.

After he put away his shot and washed it down with a swallow of beer, Boleslaw brightened. "I'm not supposed to drink."

"Who said so?"

"The doctors."

"Are they afraid it'll shorten your life?" Maud punched the old man's arm. What was Boleslaw, eighty? Somewhere in there.

"You're in a wheelchair, not on the wagon," Luke said. Boleslaw made him feel young.

The Cubs were on, and Maud changed the position of Boleslaw's chair so he could watch the game. That put her next to Luke.

"Did you call Horvath?" she asked.

"Call him what?"

Her nose wrinkled. "Meaning you didn't."

"No, and he didn't call back."

"How would you know?"

It was the kind of banter with Maud he loved, but now it seemed spoiled by what had happened in the apartment over the garage. The story had been in the *Chicago Tribune* that morning. When he saw it, he gave Maud the sports page and then put the front section behind his back.

There was a protest from Boleslaw. The bartender had changed the channel to the news mid-inning. Maud got up to tell the bartender to get the damned game back, but then she just stood there, looking at the screen. It was a story about the body found in a garage apartment in Fox River. She turned and looked at Luke.

"Later."

She sat down, still staring at him. He reached out to put his hand on her arm, but she pulled away. "Jogging!"

Well, he had run back to his car and gotten the hell out of there. It was unnerving to have Maud staring at him like that. He said again, "Later."

"Now."

The batender flipped the game back on, and Boleslaw was distracted. Luke hunched toward Maud and told her what had happened. How easy it was once he started.

Yesterday, after Melissa left, having told him she had let Greg Packer use the garage apartment, Luke seethed. He shed Maud and took the elevator to the garage to get his car. He couldn't even remember the drive to Fox River, he was so damned mad. When he pulled into the driveway, he half expected to see Greg shooting baskets, but there was no one in sight. He got out of his car and slammed the door, hard, and then went around the back of the garage. The stairway door was open, and it seemed an insult, as if the guy couldn't even close a door. The light in the stairway was on, another sign of indifference. There was a wrench halfway up the stairs; he could have stepped on it and lost his balance, broken his neck. Luke picked it up and went the rest of the way up the stairs. The door of the apartment was open, too, the son of a gun, air-conditioning the world at Luke's expense. Then he actually stumbled on the body.

He danced backward when he saw that it was Packer, eyes open but seeing nothing. His head lay in a pool of blood. Seeing a dead body in a funeral parlor, ready for viewing, was one thing, but this was a real shock. How long did he stand there, staring at the body of the guy he had driven here to throw out of this apartment? He must have thought of calling the police, he must have thought of warning Melissa, but what he did was turn and thunder back down the stairs and outside, where he realized that the wrench he was still carrying was smeared with blood. He hurled it into the weeds behind the compost heap. Then he was running down the drive to his car.

On the way back to the Loop, he thought of Melissa. Might she go up to the apartment? Good God, she mustn't get the shock he had. He should call her, but he couldn't drive and use a cell phone at the same time. Then caution, caution and fear, set in. He could hear himself ranting to Melissa that he would throw Packer out of the garage apartment. Not that she would mention that to anyone, not now, not after she learned what had happened to Packer.

When he got back to his building and pulled into the basement garage, he turned off the motor and sat behind the wheel for five minutes, trying to believe that he hadn't seen what he had seen. Then he took the elevator, holding his breath when the doors opened in the lobby—but no one got in, the doors closed, and he rose to his apartment. He changed to tennis shoes, again took the elevator to the basement, and then got outside and began to run. He did it in little bursts, ten, twenty yards, then walking, every once in a while stopping to huff and puff. How long had it been since he had run? What the hell was he doing running now? Nothing he did made a lot of sense. Still, he kept up his imitation of jogging for a couple of blocks, then turned and struggled back to the building. He came through the revolving doors to find Maud, who told him he needed a shower.

"So I took a shower," he said to her in the bar, with Boleslaw on his second boilermaker and deep in the game.

"Did anyone see you?"

"No."

"Was your daughter at home?"

"She's my daughter-in-law."

"Okay, was your daughter-in-law home?"

"Maud, I should have told her."

"Why did Horvath call?"

"What should I do?"

She sipped her beer. She was thinking. "That's the whole story?"

"So help me God."

"Do you have your phone? Call Horvath."

"What's his number?"

"I wrote it down. It's on a slip next to your phone in your apartment."

"When we go back. I need another boilermaker."

"So do I."

Boleslaw had a third, but then Maud was his designated driver.

Later, in Luke's apartment, Maud stayed with him while he called Horvath.

Sylvia Beach wore her hair in a crew cut, dyed blond, and nuts to Marco, she liked it. She suspected he did, too, though he grumbled that if he had wanted a boyfriend he would have shot himself. Macho, macho, but that was his great attraction. Sylvia had taken care of her body, and no one was going to mistake her for a boy. Marco hadn't had two consecutive thoughts in his life, at least not ones he would put into words, and that was fine with Sylvia. She'd had her fill of brooding men.

Her first impulse when she got the e-mail from Brenda Kelly was to ignore it. She didn't erase it, though, and went back and read it a couple of times. Ever since she returned to Fox River, she had thought from time to time about looking up old friends, and, of course, Brenda would have been the first. Imagine her still plugging away at what they had done working for Wally Flanagan. Sylvia had learned how to be content doing nothing, but after hooking up with Marco, it was feast or famine, out on the town in his cool sports car, hitting the spots, and then a free-for-all in bed that could last for hours. Then she wouldn't see him for a week or more, no word, no explanation; he just assumed she would be available when he was free.

"Free from what?"

He just looked at her, and his eyes went dead.

"Forget I asked."

"No, you forget you asked."

All right, all right. That was another part of his attraction, the largest part, the danger. Who had ever grown up in Fox River and not heard stories about the Pianones? Not that she had really believed the stories back then; they were just part of local lore. Marco managed two of the river craft on which gambling went on twenty-four hours a day, seven days a week. Sylvia would have liked to try her hand, but hanging around where he worked was not Marco's idea of a good time.

"You think you'd win?"

"Somebody has to win."

"That's right." He grinned.

Sylvia decided he looked like Cary Grant. She was into old movies on TCM, and there had been a week of Cary Grant. In one of them, the actor had played someone like Marco, but back in the old days when the actor still had rough edges. Maybe that's what suggested the similarity.

Over a week had gone by with no word from Marco when Sylvia tapped out a reply to Brenda. She got an answer while she was still on the computer. Brenda was all excited to learn that Sylvia was back in Fox River. When could they get together?

Sylvia called K&S and asked for Brenda Kelly.

"Speaking."

"Sylvia. What are you doing tonight?"

A squeal of delight. "Nothing! Where shall we meet?"

"I can pick you up there."

And she did, at five o'clock. Brenda hopped into Sylvia's car and then just stared. "Your hair!"

"Like it?"

It was an odd way to start a conversation after so many years. How many? They stopped for a drink and spent the first hour figuring out exactly how long it had been. Fifteen years? Geez. Brenda had put on a little weight, but she looked good, and she bubbled and babbled as if she didn't have another friend in the world.

"No husband and family?"

"Not yet."

They laughed. It seemed to restore them to the status they had both had years ago. It would only get dicey when Brenda got around to Wally. They moved from the bar to a table and ordered. A bottle of wine in the bucket next to their table, good food. It was a place Sylvia had come to with Marco. Not too smart. She didn't want to run into him here. He might think she was checking up on him. That's why, afterward, she suggested a visit to a casino, one Marco didn't manage.

They played the slots, sitting on stools amid a crowd of blue-haired ladies who fed the machines as if they were hypnotized. If this was gambling, she and Brenda decided to leave it to the addicts. So they drove back to K&S, where Brenda could get her car, and swore they would get together soon.

"We haven't even scratched the surface," Brenda said.

"I know. You haven't told me about the men in your life."

"That wouldn't take long."

"I'll bet."

A little sisterly hug, a peck on the cheek, and Brenda toddled off to her car. Sylvia watched her go, put her car in gear, and slid out of the lot. The years seemed to have taken no toll on Brenda, none at all; she was just the way she had been when they worked for Wally. By contrast, Sylvia felt that she herself had been around the block a few times.

"Not too smart," Marco said when she told him about seeing Brenda.

"Why not?"

He moved his hands, shrugged, said nothing, Maybe someday she would learn how to read his sign language. She told him about going to the casino.

"How much did you lose?"

"Why do you care?"

"I wonder how much we won."

Not too smart, he had said, and that, along with the sign language, was a message. So she wouldn't see Brenda again. It had been a miracle that they had avoided talking about Wally Flanagan. Being with Brenda had brought back the innocence of youth, the way she had been before getting mixed up with Wally. Well, she had gotten mixed up with him, and then she got wind of the blonde in the Loop. What had she expected from a married man, fidelity? Then she watched what he was doing to the blonde's account, and suspicion grew. Of course, he helped her and the other girls with their investments, but he was making Sandra Bochenski instantly rich. So she followed them, she learned where the blonde lived, and she had a chat with the little guy who opened doors at the building.

"I'm going to miss her," he said, his eyes going all over Sylvia.

She kept her shoulders back, she gave him her sweetest smile, and she learned about California. Well, by God, if Wally was taking off with a woman it was going to be her. And so it was.

When the news broke about Gregory Packer's death, Sylvia felt a chill. Every day there had been e-mails from Brenda, but they went unanswered.

"Maybe I ought to move," she suggested to Marco.

"Why?"

She reminded him about Brenda. He nodded.

"There's a building in the Loop that would work," she said.

She gave him the address, and two days later she moved. With her crew cut, she was a stranger to the doorman, and when she went by she looked right through him.

Since no relatives of Gregory Packer could be located, it had seemed that Melissa Flanagan would take responsibility, the man having been the occupant of her garage apartment when he had been slain. Then Father Dowling got a call from McDivitt, the undertaker, saying that the man's former wife would assume expenses for the funeral.

"Will you be burying him, Father?"

"I'm told he grew up in the parish."

"The body hasn't been released yet. I'll let you know."

The seniors in the parish center, for whom a funeral was, if not a festive occasion, at least a familiar one, were glad to hear that Packer would be buried from St. Hilary's. They were less than glad that Melissa had been bumped from the role of mourner in chief by Packer's former wife.

"They would have married, I'm sure of it," Lenore Holland claimed.

"They were living together, weren't they?" Gino Bacci asked.

"Oh, shush. He lived in the garage."

"What husband doesn't?"

Reproving backs were turned on Gino. This was no time for levity. In a sense, Gregory Packer had been one of them, and his death gave them the melancholy pleasure of contemplating their own.

"Let's go over to the church and say a rosary for the repose of his soul," Mimi urged.

"That can wait for the wake."

"When will it be?"

Edna assured them that Father Dowling would let them know.

Phil Keegan thought all this was going a little too far. "I suppose you'll want Cy to act as altar boy. He's the only survivor."

Marie Murkin made a wet disapproving sound. "Speak well of the dead, Captain Keegan."

"The more we find out about him, the harder that is."

Phil brought Father Dowling and the housekeeper up to date on the investigation. It had been easy to establish the cause of death, but no weapon had been found, nor were there any clues to who had managed to climb those stairs and surprise Packer from behind. The blow had been to the back of the head.

"Crushed his skull," Phil said, and Marie shuddered.

"Was it an intruder? The man was a stranger here. What enemies could he have had?"

"Oh, he had enemies enough. His second wife is dead, drowned in the pool at their home, and her nephew badgered the police to investigate, but there was nothing to investigate."

"Are you saying the nephew is an enemy?"

"The police in Laguna Beach gave details to Cy that weren't in the newspaper accounts at the time. The woman's death made

Packer the proprietor of the driving range the nephew had longed to have. I don't know if Packer was a golfer, but the nephew was. Is. You may have seen him on television playing in one of those celebrity pro-am tournaments. He couldn't make it as a pro because he had an awful temper. Broke clubs after a bad shot, or threw them into the woods. Once he whacked his caddy with a putter when the kid made a sound that caused him to miss a short putt. He was sued and settled out of court."

"What's his name?"

"Lefty Smith. Funny name. He golfed right-handed."

"Phil, you're not suggesting that Smith came to Fox River and struck down Gregory Packer, are you?"

"You wondered if he had any enemies."

"Well, that's one, if he even counts," Marie said.

"Don't forget he was in Joliet."

"So was Earl Hospers," Marie said indignantly.

"Have you made inquiries at the prison, Phil?"

"Not yet, Roger."

That night, Father Dowling dropped by the Hospers'. Earl was in the backyard, planting begonias, and the priest went out to talk to him. "You heard about Gregory Packer, Earl?"

"Edna told me."

"Had you known him?"

Earl looked up at the priest. "You mean in the place?"

"Yes."

"I knew who he was."

"Could what happened to him be connected to his time there?"

Earl patted down the earth around a just-planted begonia. "Nah. He was pretty popular. He gave golf lessons."

"Is there a golf course at Joliet?"

"There's a driving range now. Thanks to Packer."

"No enemies?"

Earl shook his head. It was obvious he did not enjoy this reminder of the long years away from his family. Father Dowling wanted to ask him if he had gardened at Joliet but decided not to.

"Oh, Earl has the touch," Edna said when he went back to the house and commented on the begonias. She leaned toward Father Dowling. "His cell was full of plants. They called him the Florist."

Amos Cadbury drove to South Bend for the Notre Dame alumni reunion, having first taken the precaution of securing a room in the Morris Inn. On one such return, he had endured several days in a residence hall and found himself unwilling to join in the more noisy evocations of past youth. The room had been far more comfortable than those he had occupied as a student, but the hubbub up and down the hall throughout the night made sleep difficult. Now, he checked in at the Morris Inn, then registered at the Alumni Center next door. Properly labeled, he ran into his old classmate Maurice Patrick in the lobby of the inn.

Patrick's name tag bounced off his enormous belly as he approached. He took Amos in his hairy arms to whisper in his ear, "We can be a twosome on what's left of Burke." He stepped back. "Six thirty okay?"

"A.M.?"

"Tomorrow."

"Wonderful."

Amos had never played the new Warren course to the north of the campus. Burke, the original course, had been reduced to nine holes, residence halls having been built on the former back nine. No course he had played since could compete with Burke for his affection, but then he had been a better golfer in those days.

He had a drink with Maurice, who seemed already to have had several, and then suggested they stroll the campus, but Maurice unfolded the reunion program. Several seminars and presentations had been checked.

"There's a discussion on the future of Notre Dame in half an hour," Maurice said, pointing to one of the checked items. "I wouldn't miss it."

Amos missed it. He was more interested in the past of the university than in its future. Like the vast majority of alumni, he was generous to his alma mater, and he leafed through the literature that arrived from South Bend with alarming regularity; what had been a secluded, rural, and all-male campus when he was there seemed to be expanding in all directions, but for him the past tense defined Notre Dame. Walking from the inn in the direction of the Main Building with the great statue of Our Lady atop its golden dome, Amos was struck by the familiarity and unfamiliarity of the place. There were at least twice as many buildings as there had been in his day.

He made his way to the Grotto, whispered a prayer for his departed wife, and then went down to the lake, where ducks and geese were everywhere. So were benches, at intervals of fifty feet. These lined the campus walks as well, each having a little bronze plaque commemorating the donor. Amos sat and looked out at the lake and thought of what he had left behind in Fox River.

The horror of coming upon the body of Gregory Packer when he had gone to tell the man that his plans for a driving range in Barrington could go forward was still with him. He had not approved of Melissa's decision to underwrite Packer's venture, knowing what Luke's reaction would be. It was difficult to think that Melissa's support could be kept a secret from her father-in-law.

"I'm going to sell the place now," Luke had said to Amos.

"But Melissa is living there."

"She won't want to stay there now."

"Luke, I can't tell you what a shock it was to discover the body."

"I know." Luke seemed to wait for his remark to register. "Amos, there is something I have to tell you."

Amos listened to Luke's account of driving angrily to Fox River to confront the unwelcome occupant of the garage apartment.

"I would have thrown him down the stairs if he had objected to leaving at once."

Amos found that he was almost indignant at this revelation. "Luke, why didn't you call the police?"

His explanation of that was halfway understandable. He had been in a rage since he heard Packer was staying in the garage apartment; he had said threatening things to Melissa, and to Maud.

"Maud."

"A woman I've come to know. A fellow resident." Luke frowned. "Can a woman be a fellow?"

"I'd have to meet her to know."

"You will, you will. Amos, there's more."

So it was that Amos heard of the bloody wrench Luke had picked up when he mounted the stairs to the garage apartment—and then the grisly discovery.

"I got out of there. It wasn't a decision, Amos, I just skedaddled. " He might have been Lord Jim explaining how he had jumped ship. "When I got to the bottom of the stairs, I realized I was still holding the wrench."

"Where is it?"

"I threw it into the weeds behind the compost heap."

"Dear God."

"What should I do, Amos?"

Now, looking out over the lake that seemed unchanged since his student days, Amos wondered if he had ever imagined in his youth that he would face such a problem as this. The wrench must surely be the murder weapon. The police investigation had so far not turned it up. Was it possible that it could lie there in the weeds undiscovered? Amos asked Luke for a more exact description of where he had thrown the wrench. That was when he made the decision that weighed so heavily on him now.

"Do nothing, Luke. It is possible it will not be found. If it is, our conversation will serve to explain what you did."

Luke slumped in his chair. "What a relief."

But Amos had felt no relief, not then, not now. Of course, he believed Luke's story. It was absurd to think that he would have used that wrench as a weapon on Gregory Packer and then come to Amos with the account he had just given. The problem was that the wrench could prove decisive in determining who had killed Gregory Packer.

Any hope Amos had that he could simply drive away from the problem and lose himself in the past on the campus of Notre Dame was dashed. For the rest of the day, he took part in a few of the planned events; he had dinner à deux with Father Hesburgh, and it was all he could do not to consult this wise old priest about his troubled conscience.

"Are you still on the advisory council at the law school, Amos?"

"No. Well, I am an emeritus member."

"And I am president emeritus." A sweet sad smile settled on the handsome visage of the man who has been called the second founder of Notre Dame. They lifted their manhattans and toasted the passage of time.

In the morning, Amos played nine holes with a hungover Maurice, taking the wheel of the cart as if he were his old classmate's designated driver. Maurice had trouble with math as he reconstructed his score on each hole and then on a par three took his driver with its enormous head, lunged at his ball, and, improbably, sent it sailing toward the green. It landed just in front, rolled toward the hole, and dropped in. They stood looking at what Maurice had done.

Maurice was too elated to crow. He just danced up and down, his eyes aglow. "That's it, Amos. I've never had a hole in one in my life before. This is my last round. I'm going to put my clubs away and dine out on that shot for the rest of my days. I only wish Packer could have seen it."

"Packer?"

"A man I took lessons from in California. At a driving range."

"Gregory Packer?"

"Do you know him?"

"I did."

"Amazing. The son of a gun owes me money. Now, I don't care."

Amos said nothing further. Back in his room, he showered and dressed for the drive back to Fox River. He had had all the reunion he could handle.

Hazel wouldn't let up about the disappearance of his client Sandra Bochenski, so Tuttle stayed away from his office. If he had been a drinking man, the occasion would have called for going on a real toot. He sat next to Mervel of the *Fox River Tribune* at the bar across from the courthouse and, watching the reporter emptying glass after glass, Tuttle felt like taking the pledge. Mervel had just come from an informal press conference across the street.

"They don't know anything," Mervel said with odd satisfaction.

"No suspects?" The fugitive thought that Melissa Flanagan might have had something to do with the death of the man she had let use the garage apartment came and went. What a tragic woman. First her husband disappeared, then his body was found in a cement mixer, and now a man had been murdered in the Flanagan garage while Melissa was living in the house. Rueful thoughts of long ago when Melissa had been his client added to Tuttle's melancholy. How much had she been told of the woman Wally Flanagan had planned to meet in California and begin a new life with, living in sin together? Tuttle was not given to moralizing, but marital infidelity was one thing he condemned unequivocally. His parents had provided him with a model of what marriage should be, steady and loving and undramatic, until death do us part. Perhaps he himself had never married because he knew he could not realize that ideal. Imagine being tied down to someone like Hazel. He shuddered.

"Have another," Mervel advised.

"I'm still working on this one." Tuttle's Guinness was still half full. Or half empty. Or both.

"There must have been a falling-out," Mervel said.

"What do you mean?"

"Mrs. Flanagan and the dead guy."

"No way."

Mervel snickered. "Cherchez the floozy. That's still the best rule."

"You're drunk," Tuttle said angrily, getting off his stool.

"Not yet."

Tuttle threw a couple of bills on the counter and turned to go. He was called back. He was short two bucks. How the devil could Mervel afford to drink in this place? But then he was running a tab.

He was still angry at Mervel for his slur on Melissa Flanagan when he crossed the street. Before he reached the opposite curb, he was nearly run over. He danced out of harm's way and then saw Peanuts Pianone behind the wheel of the car that had almost hit him. Tuttle opened the passenger door and hopped in. "You missed."

"The Great Wall?"

"Where else."

In the restaurant, with their table covered with dishes of Oriental delicacies, Peanuts settled down to feeding himself.

"Anything new on Gregory Packer, Peanuts?"

Peanuts shrugged. "Someone bonked him on the head. A messy job."

Suddenly Peanuts sat upright. He looked around, then frowned at Tuttle.

"You got a cell phone, Peanuts?"

Eureka. A sly smile. He plucked a phone from his pocket and studied it as it went on buzzing. Then he punched a button and put it to his ear. "Yeah."

Peanuts glowered as he listened, repeated "yeah" several times, and then returned the phone to his pocket.

"What is it?"

"Lucky bitch."

"Who?" Of course, he didn't have to ask. The only woman other than Hazel who stirred Peanuts to contempt was Agnes Lamb, the black officer, many years his junior on the force. Agnes had long since eclipsed Peanuts—not a great feat in itself, but Tuttle had heard both Phil Keegan and Cy Horvath praise the young officer. "Agnes Lamb?"

Peanuts uttered an uncharacteristic profanity.

"Lucky how?"

"She thinks she found the murder weapon."

"Who called you?"

A repetition of the profanity. "She wants me there. With the car."

Tuttle, of course, went along to the Flanagan house, expecting to find patrol cars all over the place, but there was no one in evidence. Peanuts bounced in the driveway and slammed on the brakes. When Tuttle got out, a voice called from above. Agnes Lamb was looking out a window in the apartment above the garage.

Peanuts stayed in the car, but Tuttle went around behind the garage and up the stairs and knocked on the apartment door.

Agnes opened it. "Where is everybody?" she asked.

"Who?"

"Keegan, Horvath, anybody. No one is in. I told them to put it on the radio. So I called whatchamacallit." Meaning Peanuts. Agnes crossed the living room and picked up the phone.

"How did you get here?"

"A cab. I had an idea, Yo-yo out there had our car, so I took a cab. And I was right."

"About what?"

"Wait till the lab gets here."

Agnes dialed and this time was successful. A crew was on its way. When it arrived, Peanuts continued to sit behind the wheel of the car, brooding like Achilles in his tent. Tuttle followed the crew, who followed Agnes into the backyard, beyond the compost pile, where she pointed. Tuttle pressed forward and got a glimpse of the wrench scarcely visible in the weeds.

*　*　*

Photographs of the scene were being taken when Cy Horvath showed up. He looked down at the wrench and gave orders to have the wrench taken to the lab.

He put his arm around Agnes. "Good work," he said.

"It's a living," Regis McDivitt replied whenever he was asked what it was like being an undertaker. His father had always told him that they were engaged in one of the corporal works of mercy—burying the dead—but, of course, McDivitt's and other funeral parlors made a pretty good thing of it. Regis was the third generation of McDivitts who had prepared the departed for viewing and conducted them to the church for their funeral Mass and then on to the cemetery to their final resting place. The occupation should have induced long thoughts on the contingency of existence and the inevitability of death, but Regis went about his work with a cheerful insouciance, despondent with the sad, even-tempered with the stoics, bubbly with those who seemed to think of death as a swift passage to fun and games elsewhere. The main thing was to be all things to all men.

In the case of the final obsequies of Gregory Packer, it was difficult to know what audience one was playing to. Death by violence was rarer than one would think, at least in Regis's experience, but when it occurred one was prepared for unbridled grief and showy despair from the survivors. But who were Gregory Packer's survivors? There were no relatives, and any friends he had seemed to be of recent vintage.

"Mass of the Angels?" Regis asked Father Dowling.

"No, I think a requiem Mass."

"Good for you." The words just came, and Regis backed away lest Father Dowling take offense. Apparently not. You have to be careful with the clergy, an edgy bunch, usually on their dignity. Dowling was unusual, though. McDivitt's had secured a monopoly of St. Hilary's funerals before Dowling's time at the cost of free calendars with saccharine reproductions of religious art of the worst sort and, of course, the name, address, and telephone number of McDivitt, your friendly undertaker.

Although it was a preference expressed only in the privacy of his own mind, Regis preferred an old-fashioned funeral, Latin if possible, the *Dies Irae*, black vestments, a seemly sense of the desolation involved in the death of a human being. Dowling said the rosary at the wake at McDivitt's, and there was a satisfactory turnout, the folding chairs filled with the old people who hung out at the St. Hilary senior center. Regis, assuming his all-purpose expression, loitered in the back of the viewing room, happy that there was a minimum of chatter and an appropriate gloom over the assembly.

Cy Horvath came up beside Regis. "Good turnout."

"Of course." The death of Gregory Packer had been a prominent item in the local news during a slack period. Where the body is found, there the eagles will gather—or words to that effect.

The Flanagans had been ushered to the front row: Luke,

Melissa, and a cheery little woman who seemed to be with Luke. Regis had put Sandra Bochenski in the front row across the aisle from the Flanagans.

Father Dowling had taken up his position on the kneeler in front of the open casket and begun the sorrowful mysteries when Tuttle the lawyer came in, wearing his signature tweed hat. Regis glared at it, and Tuttle removed it. He looked over the assembly and then headed down the aisle, stopping at the front row left, then taking a chair beside Sandra Bochenski.

Cy recognized the woman Tuttle had joined as the onetime love of Wally Flanagan. Then he was immediately distracted by the entrance of another couple. The man was Marco Pianone, but Cy did not recognize the woman. They settled into a back row. Marco Pianone! The last time Cy had seen Marco at a funeral had been a four-star send-off for a man who had likely been a victim of the family omertà.

Five minutes later, Brenda Kelly came in, standing in the doorway for a moment until she recognized Cy. She came to stand beside him. "I'm late."

No later than Gregory Packer.

"Where's Mrs. Flanagan?" Brenda asked.

"Front row, right side."

Brenda craned her neck to get a better look. "Beautiful as ever."

"Take a pew."

"I don't have a rosary."

Regis produced one as if by magic and handed it to her, courtesy of McDivitt's Funeral Home. Brenda started toward the chairs but, recognizing Marco and his companion, scooted to the opposite side. Cy wished he had asked Brenda who the woman with Marco was.

Marco was a distracting presence, inviting thoughts of how the body of Wally Flanagan had been found. Being found piecemeal in a cement mixer suggested the Pianone touch. Why would Marco show up for the wake of Gregory Packer?

Father Dowling said one mystery kneeling, the next standing, to make it easier on the mourners. Marco had produced a huge rosary, the beads looking like jewels, the crucifix massive. His presence seemed a statement, but Cy could not read its meaning.

Tuttle had thought he would have to crawl over Sandra Bochenski to the empty seat to her left, but she moved in, and that gave him the advantage, in case he wanted to bolt. He stole a glance at her and saw that her eyes were full of tears. After what she had told him of Packer's treatment of her, the tears should have been of the crocodile sort, but they seemed genuine. That diminished his anger at the way she had seemed to have given him the slip.

Father Dowling finished the rosary, stood, and turned, and then people began to come forward to kneel on the prie-dieu and get a good look at the embalmed deceased.

"You checked out of the Whitehall," Tuttle said out of the side of his mouth.

"I left a message with your assistant."

"I didn't get it."

"When can we get together?"

This was disarming. Maybe she hadn't meant to dodge her responsibility to her professional advisor.

"Where did you go from the Whitehall?

For answer, she took a card from her purse and gave it to him. Tuttle had his tweed hat on his lap. He deposited the card in it.

"Will you be at the funeral tomorrow?" She asked him.

"Of course."

"We'll talk afterward. There are things you should know."

Regis McDivitt had slipped off to his office and the consolations of a mild bourbon and water. He toasted the photograph of his grandfather, the founder, and sipped complacently. You could count on Father Dowling to make things run smoothly. Not even the presence of Marco Pianone in his viewing room could upset Regis tonight. A pretty good turnout for a rolling stone; of course, it was the contingent from the St. Hilary senior center that filled the room. They knew how to say the rosary. In his line of work, Regis could not help but notice the fall-off of such pious practices. He kept a large supply of inexpensive rosaries on hand, since by and large people didn't carry one with them nowadays. They kept them, by and large, maybe even got back into the habit of using them. Regis felt a little bit like a missionary, bringing Catholicism to Catholics. Not that he would say such a thing out loud. An undertaker was by definition a background figure, seen but not heard, the reassurance that since these grim occasions were for him almost daily fare, this one would go well.

12

Cy's wife, Fran, wanted a blow-by-blow account of the wake for Gregory Packer—who was there, who said what to whom, was Regis still sucking mints.

"It was a wake. There's a body, you say some prayers and get out of there."

"Come on. Were the Flanagans there?"

"The Flanagans were there. You're this curious, why didn't you come along?"

"I hate wakes."

She hated funerals, too, so Cy went alone the following morning for the ten o'clock funeral Mass. Of course, he was on duty. They had six of the old guys from the center acting as pallbearers, and even then Regis had to give them a hand.

It was pretty much the same bunch as the night before, except that Marco wasn't there. Fran had a cat that liked hanging around the picture window of the house next door, driving the dog in the house crazy. To have the enemy so near and yet so far. Any Pianone but Peanuts was like that cat so far as Cy was concerned. The enemy you couldn't get at. It was still a puzzle why Marco had come to the wake.

"That was Sylvia with him," Brenda said when he asked her.

"That explains his coming?"

"He came with her."

"Okay, why did she come?"

"Ask me why I did."

Cy asked, and she told him. She and Sylvia had worked for Wally Flanagan; the dead man had been living in the garage apartment at the Flanagan home.

"That's it?"

"Don't you see?"

"Where did you flunk logic?"

"I wish she'd answer my e-mails." Another convoluted explanation followed this.

"So give her a call, write her a letter."

Brenda drew closer. "She's not in the book. I don't know where she lives."

"I have an idea."

"What?"

"Ask her."

By then Sylvia had left.

After the Mass, most of the seniors went back to the center, and there was only a small group at the cemetery, which made the three women, Brenda, Sylvia, and Sandra, all the more conspicuous. Sandra had widow status, in a way, but the other two must just like funerals. Tuttle was sticking to Sandra Bochenski like a bill collector. The casket had been placed on rollers and positioned over the open grave, effectively concealing it unless you were standing close. Rugs of artificial grass had been laid over the dirt that had come from the hole. Father Dowling, in street clothes, read from a book and sprinkled holy water on the casket, and that was it. The casket would be lowered into the grave and covered over after they left.

Cy loped across the incline to his car. He got the news from downtown before he was halfway out of the cemetery.

"The only fingerprints on the wrench are Luke Flanagan's," Agnes told him, excitement in her voice.

"So what?"

"So what? Did you hear me? His fingerprints are on what Dr. Pippen and others are sure was the murder weapon."

"Agnes, it was his house, his garage, no doubt his wrench."

"Cy, these are fresh prints. Very fresh."

If he had shared Agnes's excitement, he would have turned around and gone back to ask Luke about it.

"How fresh?"

"Talk to the lab," Agnes said, disgusted. She hung up before he could say anything else.

Phil Keegan thought the fingerprints significant, too. "We've got nothing else, Cy."

"You want me to talk to Luke?"

"Not yet. Agnes is going to see if she can find out where Luke was when Packer was killed."

"We could find that out by talking to Luke."

Phil shook his head. "Of course, it's a long shot. If he was in the Loop at the time, the fingerprints don't mean a thing."

By the Loop, Phil meant the place where Luke lived, just off the Magnificent Mile. Cy got Agnes on the radio and told her he would meet her there.

Agnes was in the lobby talking to the woman who had sat next to Luke at the wake. Her name was Maud. She looked Cy over appraisingly. "You're a big son of a gun."

"I saw you at the wake."

She laughed. "Where else are you going to see a woman my age?"

"But you didn't go to the funeral."

"The next burial I go to will be my own. I've seen too much of it."

Agnes was getting impatient with all this banter. "Mrs. Lynn," she broke in.

"Maud."

"Maud, we're here because we're following routine. Could I ask you a few questions?"

"Shoot. And I don't mean with that." She pointed at Agnes's weapon. Agnes was in uniform.

Cy let Agnes ask the questions, a little too bluntly maybe, but all of them to the point. She told Maud the approximate time of Packer's death and explained that the routine was meant to establish where everybody was at that time.

"I was right here."

"Okay. Good. And Luke Flanagan?"

"He lives here, too."

"I know that. Were you together?"

"Sweetie, we've become inseparable."

"Right here?"

"Right here. Well, in his room." She dipped her head and looked at Agnes over her glasses.

"Okay, okay." She thanked Maud and asked her how she liked living there.

"You call this living?"

"You should see my place."

Maud was lying, Cy would have bet his badge on it, but why? She wasn't protecting herself, so it must be Luke she was lying for. Cy watched Maud continue to wrap Agnes around her finger.

The elevator door slid open, and a man in a wheelchair pushed himself into the lobby. His face lit up when he saw Maud, and he rolled up beside her. "Can we go for a beer?"

"Not right now, Boleslaw." Cy had moved toward the wheelchair, and Maud looked up at him. "This is Boleslaw Bochenski."

"Bochenski?"

The old man glared at Cy.

"Where do you go for a beer?"

Maud told him of the bar up the street.

"I'll take you," Cy said."I could use a beer myself."

So he got Bochenski through the revolving doors, a bit of a trick, and rolled him up the street to the bar Maud had mentioned.

Inside it was about thirty degrees cooler than outside, but it seemed a nice place. Cy got them settled at a table, and a waitress came over.

"A boilermaker," the old man said.

"Make it two."

While they waited, the old man peered at Cy. "Do I know you?"

"My name is Horvath. I'm a cop in Fox River. I know your daughter."

"Daughter? Do I have a daughter?"

"Sandra."

"She called yesterday. I haven't seen her for years."

"She's been in California."

"So she said."

Their drinks came, and Cy dropped the subject. The old man was more interested in the ball game than in his daughter anyway. Between innings, though, he leaned toward Cy. "She moved me into that place. She pays for it. She's not all bad."

Boleslaw was on his second boilermaker when Luke Flanagan joined them.

"Maud says you were looking for me."

"One question, Luke. Where were you on Wednesday afternoon?"

"I thought so."

"What do you mean?"

"Did someone see me leave?"

"Tell me about it."

Luke's story was the twin of Amos Cadbury's, only he had been in the garage apartment before the lawyer, and he had threatened to throw Packer out of the garage apartment on his ear. For years he had blamed Packer for the fact that Wally had not turned out as Luke had hoped.

"We found the wrench, Luke."

"Have a boilermaker," Boleslaw urged Luke.

"Do I have time?" Luke asked.

"I'll have another myself."

The arrest of Luke Flanagan on suspicion of murder put Amos Cadbury in a delicate position, and he drove himself out to St. Hilary's to talk with Father Dowling. "They've arrested Luke Flanagan."

"Yes."

"Father, I may have done a stupid thing."

"I doubt that, Amos."

"It's true that I don't regret it."

"Tell me."

They sat in the pastor's study, the door closed against the curiosity of Marie Murkin. Amos unwrapped a cigar and prepared it lovingly. When he applied a match to it and turned it slowly, ensuring an even burn, it was a work of art.

"Luke came to me and told me that he had gone out to his old house to throw Packer out of the garage apartment. He said he came upon a scene very much like the one I came upon."

"Do you mean he found Packer already dead?"

"I believed him. I do believe him. On the way up the stairs, he picked up something he had stumbled on. It turned out to be the wrench that killed Packer. Luke fled in a panic, and when he got outside, he threw the wrench into the backyard, where it was found."

"That accounts for his fingerprints on it."

Father Dowling remembered Melissa sitting in this study, telling him that she had made a big mistake in allowing Packer to use the garage apartment. He told Amos that.

"On the very day it happened?"

"Yes."

"Good Lord, Father, what if she had gone home and surprised the intruder?" The old lawyer closed his eyes at the thought.

"She spoke of helping Packer set himself up in business."

"Yes, a driving range. We had talked about that, Melissa and I. He had an appointment to see me when I was to give him the good news. Of course, I saw it largely as a way to get him away from her. Once he had the money, he wouldn't have any reason to linger, but he didn't show up for the appointment." Amos paused. "You'll forgive me if I say that was an uncommon experience for me. I drove out there in anger, much as Luke himself had earlier."

"Packer's experience with driving ranges hadn't been good."

"What experience of his had been? When he wept at Wallace's funeral, I liked the man. Everyone else turned it into some sort of pep rally, even . . . But I must not criticize the Franciscans."

Father Dowling smiled. Amos had an old-fashioned conception of the deference due the clergy.

"Now, if they persist in seeing Luke as the assailant, I will have to come forward and testify in his behalf. I assured him at the time that he had been wise to tell me, not that I thought he would become a suspect."

"Wouldn't that come under lawyer/client privilege?"

"Of course."

"What a star-crossed family the Flanagans are."

"Indeed, indeed. The sins of the son visited on the father."

Edna, when Father Dowling had talked to her before the discovery of Packer's body, had expressed annoyance at Melissa.

"What else did she suppose people would think? The two of them were inseparable here, Father, but to let him move into that apartment—" Edna made a face. "Is she really that naive?"

"What is Packer like?"

"He's a man." Then Edna laughed. "A real charmer."

"So Marie assures me."

"What on earth does he live on? He had no job. He's too young for Social Security. I suppose he was mooching off Melissa."

"Where did he live before he moved to the garage apartment."

"A motel." She paused. "The Tiger Lily."

"That's its name?"

"Not the most wholesome place."

When he mentioned the motel to Phil Keegan, his old friend sat back. "That was a Pianone operation. Maybe it still is."

"Meaning?"

"Drugs, women, the lot."

"I'm surprised that a man on parole was permitted to stay there."

"Don't get me started, Roger. Most parole officers are convinced their clients were the victims of injustice and are incapable of wrongdoing. If someone has never done anything wrong, he can scarcely relapse."

"It sounds like he's better off not living in such a place."

"But was Melissa Flanagan better off having him living in her garage apartment?"

The next day, Melissa came to the rectory. Marie treated her with deference, put her in the front parlor, and informed Father Dowling in lowered tones who had come to see him.

When he went to the parlor, she was sitting in a chair, looking out the window. She turned to him, her eyes wide with horror. "Father, what have I done?"

She seemed to think that by offering Packer the garage apartment, she had put him in harm's way. Father Dowling soothed her, assuring her that she had performed an act of kindness.

"Try to convince my father-in-law of that. Oh, the poor man. I seem to have brought him nothing but tragedy and sorrow."

She had cast herself in the role of nemesis to her family and friends. She wished that she had never come back to Fox River.

"Did Gregory ever say anything to suggest he was in danger?"

"No." As soon as she said it, second thoughts seemed to come. "He had spent time in prison, you know."

"I have heard he was very popular there."

"Of course, he would have been."

"So he never suggested that he had any enemies."

"Only his first wife."

"How so?"

"I didn't want to hear the story, not really. It was sordid. They met and married in a matter of weeks, and almost immediately he regretted it. She deserted him, absconding with all their savings. You always hear of husbands abusing their wives, but in their case it was the reverse. He told me he sometimes feared she would kill him."

In the silence that followed, that reported threat from the past and what had happened in the Flanagan garage apartment seemed two ends of the same thought.

"Did he ever say where she is now?"

"Somewhere in California. That's why he came back here. To troubles of a different kind, as it turned out, and then . . ."

This seemed information Phil Keegan should have, and Father Dowling asked Melissa if she would mind his passing it along.

Phil nodded. "Cy has tracked down his first wife."

"In California?"

"Oh, she's back in the Chicago area."

The two men sat looking at each other.

"Cy will follow up on that, Father."

Maud realized how close she had become to Luke now that he was staying with his daughter-in-law in the house he had built for his family in Fox River. She called him every day and urged him to come see her.

"I'm bad luck, Maud."

"I know that. I'm tired of good luck."

"Now you can flirt with Boleslaw."

It was good to hear that barking laugh again.

"I could come see you."

"You wouldn't be able to find it."

"Being lost in Fox River sounds better than being found in Chicago. Or vice versa."

As it turned out, he arranged for his nephew Frank Looney to pick her up and drive her to Fox River.

"What's it like living there?" Frank Looney asked when they set off.

"One mad whirl from morning to night."

"No kidding?"

That might have been his motto. He was an earnest man in his forties without a whisper of a sense of humor. Once that was established, she gave him a straightforward account of life in Stalag 17. This designation puzzled him.

"Your uncle calls it that." She went on to tell him it was a World War II POW camp.

"A prison?"

"That's right."

Luke's jokes were bad enough unexplained, but the mention of prison cast a pall over the conversation.

"So you run Flanagan Concrete."

Here was a topic he could handle. For the rest of the drive, she heard about how well the business was doing and the innovations he had made ("Always with Uncle Luke's approval"). He thought he had inherited his uncle's Midas touch, if turning sand and other things into cement was comparable to changing things into gold. This was Maud's unexpressed caveat.

"How many trucks do you have?"

She got an inventory of the business, the jobs they were on now, the prospects for the future. Maud was glad when they got to the house.

"I better get back to the yard," Frank said when his uncle came out to greet Maud.

"Maybe I'll keep her here."

"I understand you have an empty apartment," Maud deadpanned.

Frank just stared at the two of them and then got out of there.

"What a witty nephew you have."

"He's what you get when your sister marries a Looney. Not too smart but reliable. The business is in good hands."

They stood facing one another. He was obviously glad to see her, so why didn't he make a move?

"Shake," she said, thrusting out her hand.

They were hand in hand when Melissa came out. She beamed at them and then, apparently remembering the cloud Luke was under, looked sad.

Maud got a tour of the house—quite a mansion; she wouldn't have imagined Luke building such a place, let alone living in it. No wonder he had moved to Stalag 17.

"I raised my family here," Luke said, following along as Melissa showed Maud around.

"I don't want any more children."

"How's Boleslaw?"

"Hell on wheels."

"Who's Boleslaw?" Melissa asked.

"That's her boyfriend."

"I think he prefers you."

They ended up in the kitchen after Luke said the front room was for company. Coffee and gingersnaps.

"Is this a no smoking area?"

"Light up, Maud."

Melissa sat across the table from them with the silliest smile on her face. Maud wondered if she came with the house.

Later, in the living room, she was shown the family photographs on the mantel. She studied one. "Remember that man I told you I met in Kentucky? Put a beard on this face, and they could be cousins."

"That's my son, Wally. He's dead."

Maud observed a moment of silence. "And this is your first wife?"

"They threw away the mold."

"My husband thought I was pretty moldy, too."

Luke had his arm around her hips. She lifted it higher. "Watch it."

After Melissa left them alone, they quit the banter and talked about his troubles.

"They actually think I did it, Maud."

"Well, you know better."

"They're down to two suspects."

"Two."

"It's me or Melissa."

He showed her the article by Mervel in the local paper. It read like a bad Sherlock Holmes story, pure speculation. Except, of course, for the wrench.

"That's what made you Public Enemy Number One?"

Mervel had been told about the rubber gloves in the apartment's kitchen sink. Someone—it was clear the someone was Melissa—could have worn gloves when she wielded the wrench.

"Show me the scene of the crime."

"Are you serious?"

"Do you think I came all the way out here just to see you?"

"All right."

They went out a side door and toward the garage. The area was marked off with yellow tape. There was a cop on duty who stirred into life at their approach. He moved over when Luke tried to go around him. "I can't let you go up there."

"Hey, I own the place."

"I'm sorry. It's still off-limits."

Maud said, "Not only is he the owner, he's the chief suspect."

Luke waved her off. "You don't object if we go into the garage, do you?"

"Not upstairs."

"The garage."

"Go ahead."

Once inside, he lowered the door again. It was warm and musty and poorly lit.

"Alone at last," Maud said.

"Come on. I want to show you something."

He led her between the cars to a workbench along the back wall. Tools were neatly arranged over it; there were containers of screws and nails and staples. Luke pointed to the ceiling, from which dangled a rope with a wooden handle attached. He pulled it, and a door in the ceiling dropped open. A switch over the workbench activated the metal ladder that began to descend from the opened door, section by section. When it reached the garage floor, Luke did things to its sides to make them rigid.

"I'll go first. I'm not wearing a skirt."

"I noticed that."

They emerged into a pantry off the kitchen of the apartment, where Luke explained about the alternative entry.

"When this apartment was being designed, Wally was a teenager, always reading crazy stories. He proposed this ladder exit. We may have been the first ones to use it in twenty years. It was the only way Wally ever went up here." As Luke spoke, his face lit up with those memories. He stopped. "And Wally's dead. Come on, I'll show you around."

So she saw where the body had lain, and looked down the stairway on which Luke had found the bloody wrench.

Melissa drove Maud back to Chicago, and they talked about Luke's troubles. Not that Melissa thought her father-in-law was in any trouble.

"Of course, he should have reported what he found, but in a way he did. He went to Amos Cadbury and told him the whole story."

"He shouldn't have picked up that wrench."

"He tripped over it. It was perfectly natural to pick it up."

Melissa was so sure Luke was innocent that she made him sound guilty. Not that Maud didn't admire the younger woman's loyalty.

"I should have given him an alibi, said we were smooching in my room at the time and he made up that story to protect my name."

"Because of the time? But that's nonsense. They have to take *my* word for where I was at the time."

"Where were you?"

"I told them I was talking with a priest." A laughing Melissa changed lanes, passed a semi, and then got back in the fast lane.

Maud wondered if Luke really was in trouble. She wondered more what she could do for him. That was when she decided to visit her son the monk. Maybe God would hear her prayers better if she sent them up from a Trappist monastery.

When Tuttle entered the building, a little guy in a uniform came out from behind a kind of pulpit and stood in his path. "Where you going?"

"That's some uniform." The lawyer put out a hand. "Tuttle. Of Tuttle and Tuttle."

The hand had made the guy dance backward, but now he took it warily. "Ferret. Who you want to see?"

"Sandra Bochenski."

"What's Tuttle and Tuttle?"

"The largest law firm in Fox River."

Tuttle didn't like Ferret's laugh, but he joined in. Elementary strategy. If Ferret blocked the elevator, he would have to telephone his client and tell her he was in the lobby. If she still was his client.

"What's she need a lawyer for?"

"She's bringing charges against you."

Ferret's eyes widened, then narrowed. "Don't I wish. Geez, it's good to have her back in the building."

"Did she get her old place back?"

"Are you kidding? No, she's subletting. Got the place for a couple months."

"You knew her before?"

Ferret nodded, then looked beyond Tuttle. Someone had come through the revolving doors. The man sailed past Tuttle and Ferret without so much as looking at them, went to the elevator and punched a button, and then waited with obvious impatience until the doors slid open and he entered.

When the elevator door closed, Ferret looked at Tuttle and shook his head. "This was always a class place, but now?" He shook his head again. "He stashed his bimbo here."

"Who is he?"

"Damned if I know."

Tuttle knew. It was Marco Pianone. The woman Ferret called a bimbo was Sylvia Beach. Tuttle thought about that on the way up in the elevator.

Sandra was in a housecoat, her hair wild, a glass of orange juice in her hand. "I thought you said you'd call first."

"The battery on my cell phone must be dead."

The apartment was in the front of the building with a view of the lake. She offered Tuttle coffee, but when he accepted she said she would make some.

"Is that orange juice?"

So they drank orange juice while she explained to him why she no longer needed his services.

"Because Gregory Packer is dead?"

"What's the point of finding out if he was responsible for what happened to Wally? I think he was involved in some way, he had to be, but what difference does it make now?"

"I hate loose ends."

Sitting in this lovely apartment gave Tuttle the sensation that his career had entered a new and affluent phase, but she was telling him it was all over. On the edge of his mind, he was trying to figure out the significance of Marco Pianone's stashing his bimbo in this building. The Pianones had certainly come up in the world. In the past, their bimbos would have been housed in places like the Tiger Lily motel, not on the Gold Coast of Chicago.

"Had you found out anything?"

"Let me put it this way. When you heard Packer was dead, who was the first one you thought might have done it?"

"Me!"

"You?"

"Let me tell you a little secret." She clutched her housecoat to her breast. "That garage apartment? Wally and I used to go there sometimes. Have you ever seen it? It's nicer than this place. There we were, his father only a short distance off in the big house, snug as bugs in a rug." A wistful smile crossed her face like clouds across the sky. "He said he felt like a kid again in that apartment, before his life got complicated, before he got married. There's a secret entrance, you know."

"Secret."

"Through the garage, a trapdoor and ladder. We always got into and out of the apartment that way." She went on to describe that second way into the garage apartment. The memory seemed to brighten her.

"That would have enabled you to get up there and catch Packer unawares?"

"Oh, it wasn't me who killed him."

"Of course not. So who could it have been?"

She looked at him reflectively. "Maybe I would still like you to find out what you can."

"Good."

"Have you found out anything?" she asked again.

Tuttle thought of the lobby, he thought of Ferret, he thought of . . .

"What do you know of the Pianone family?"

"Good Lord."

"You've heard of them."

"Wally had all kinds of gory stories about them. I didn't know whether to believe him or not. Once, he said that maybe they were the answer to his problem."

"What problem?"

"His wife. Of course, he was just kidding, but when we were up in that apartment above the garage, we were both like teenagers, plotting against the adults. Sometimes I wish we had just left things as they were then. He'd be alive, I would never have met Greg . . ."

Her voice trailed away, and Tuttle realized that she might be sitting on top of the world in one sense, in this apartment, and was still a good-looking woman, but she was all alone.

"You've got this place for how long?"

"Just a few months. I'm going to have to decide on my future during that time." She looked toward the lake. "My father is not half a mile from here."

"No kidding."

"In a retirement home. Not that it looks like one. The building is pretty much like this one. It's the least I can do for him, not that he ever did much for me. A funny thing. The newspaper stories about Wally's father? He lives there, too."

"A small world."

"What about the Pianones?"

"Why don't I hold that until I learn more?"

Ferret was out on the sidewalk having a smoke, cupping the cigarette as if he were engaged in an illegal act. Maybe he was. He held it behind him when Tuttle went over to him.

"When did the bimbo get stashed here?"

"I'm sorry I told you."

"It will go easier for you because you did."

"You sound like a cop."

"I'm a lawyer."

"That's worse."

"You may be right. Keep the faith."

Tuttle went jauntily up the street. He still had a client. He was so elated that he even considered calling Hazel and letting her know—but why spoil such a wonderful day?

16

As Melissa Flanagan had insisted, she had as much opportunity as her father-in-law to kill Gregory Packer, but there were several things wrong with that. She had no motive, and it turned out that she had been at St. Hilary's talking with Father Dowling more or less at the crucial time.

"Cyril, you know how close St. Hilary's is to the Flanagan house."

"I was raised in that parish."

"Then you know I could have seen Father Dowling and gone back to the house, before or after, during that stretch of time."

The more she insisted, the guiltier she made Luke look. Even so, it was a nice gesture, throwing herself on her sword for her father-in-law. Jacuzzi, the prosecutor, was eager to get moving against Luke Flanagan.

"Motive we got, but who cares, we've got the weapon, and we've got his admission he was there. His prints are all over the wrench. He threw it away. We were lucky to find it."

"We?"

Jacuzzi ignored this. "Murder is hard to make stick, so we go for manslaughter."

Robertson, the chief, was equally eager, saying that they didn't want to be accused of favoritism because Luke Flanagan was such a big man in the construction world in Fox River. The chief's eagerness was enough to get Phil Keegan to dig in his heels. Robertson was, of course, a political appointee, a lousy cop who had been made chief ten years ago, but politics in Fox River meant the Pianones.

"Why would they set up Luke Flanagan, Cy?"

Cy looked at his boss, but the disappointment he felt did not make it into his unchanged expression. No one was less happy about the mess Luke Flanagan was in than Cy, but if this became a pro- and anti-Pianone struggle, they were going to lose. "The Pianones didn't drive him out to his old house, Phil."

"The wrench, Cy. The wrench. The only fresh prints on it are Luke's. He has an explanation for that."

"What if he hadn't picked it up? There'd be no case."

"That was dumb, sure."

"Meaning no one planned it, Phil. He wasn't set up."

"You think he killed Packer?"

"I think we better find out who did or Luke is going to trial."

"That's been your assignment all along."

Whatever had happened to Greg Packer seemed connected to the disappearance and death of Wally Flanagam years ago. Cy didn't know how, and he had been trained not to rely on hunches, but that was the hunch he had. So Cy went back to K&S to talk with Brenda Kelly.

Her head dawned over the counter, a phone pressed to her ear. She smiled and waggled her fingers, indicating it wouldn't be a sec. She made a face when she put down the phone. "The Dow went down yesterday. You'd think it was the *Titanic*."

"We need to talk."

"Wanna go for coffee?"

"How about lunch?"

"Great. I'll save the one I brought for tomorrow."

He took her to the Great Wall. She began to sing something from *The Mikado* when he asked her if she liked Chinese.

"Isn't that Japanese?"

"They all look alike."

"Careful, careful."

They ordered, their food came, and they began to eat. While they ate, they talked about Sylvia.

"She didn't go on with you to K and S, so where did she work?"

"Oh, she left town."

"Don't tell me she went to California."

"Oh, no. Minnesota."

"Minnesota? Why Minnesota?"

Brenda took a bite of an egg roll, watching him as she chewed. "Why all the questions?"

He developed it for her, against all his rules, a little possible scenario. Wally Flanagan had planned to go off with one woman, at least that's what he told her, but then he disappeared. He never showed up in California. Sylvia left town. "Maybe she and Wally went off together."

"Do you think I didn't think of that?"

"Did you ask her?"

"How could I just ask a thing like that?"

"What you could do is find out where in Minnesota she lived."

"There's only one problem, I can't get in touch with her. I don't have a phone number, and she doesn't answer my e-mails. That's how I got in touch with her before. By e-mail. When I saw her at the wake, I tried to talk with her, but she and her man just buzzed out of there."

So that went nowhere. With all the cooperation in the world from Minnesota police, it would be a difficult thing to find out where Sylvia Beach had spent those years. If she did go off with Wally, what name would he have used? Cy remembered the suspicion he had when they first turned up that California marriage license with Gregory Packer as groom. Well, Gregory Packer had been Gregory Packer, not Wally Flanagan. So he asked colleagues in Minneapolis to see if they could turn up a Gregory Packer living in the state up until a few years ago. It was like dropping money down a well—but two days later he got a message. A Gregory Packer had lived just outside Garrison, Minnesota. He looked it up. Garrison was way up in the North Woods. He got in touch with the county sheriff and faxed him a photo of Wally Flanagan. In a matter of hours he had confirmation. The picture was of the Gregory Packer who had lived near Garrison.

"How the hell did you find that out?" Phil Keegan said, obviously delighted.

"Just routine investigating."

"Good work."

So now they knew where Wally Flanagan had spent those years. Now, if he could only get hold of Sylvia Beach, he could fill in the picture. She ought to know what had brought him back to Fox River all those years ago, presuming he had arrived alive.

Agnes Lamb had made it as a cop, as a detective. Phil Keegan knew it; even more important, Cy Horvath knew it; and above all, she knew it. At first it was only that she was better than Peanuts Pianone, but that wasn't saying much. Peanuts was a constant reminder of the limits within which they worked, thanks to the influence of the Pianone family and more proximately because of the fact that said family had Chief Robertson in its pocket. That was one constraint. Another was the untouchables, people with such standing in the community that they were treated with kid gloves. Agnes did not know which of these two constraints grated on her more.

Jacuzzi was anxious to move forward and bring Luke Flanagan to trial, but now Robertson advised caution. After all, Flanagan was a self-made zillionaire, and even if he had moved to a posh retirement community in Chicago, he remained a Fox River biggie. Also, there was the tragedy of Wallace Flanagan, which remained as a great mute rebuke to the department. They had been unable to locate Luke's son when he was missing, and when he turned up dead in one of the Flanagan cement mixers he went into the bulging file of unsolved murders. Ever since she had found that wrench in the weeds at the back of the Flanagan property and the lab had identified the prints on it as Luke's, Agnes had closed the case in her mind. Almost.

Of course, Luke Flanagan said he was innocent, even though he had volunteered the story that he had been at the garage apartment, discovered the body of Gregory Packer, and then fled. He hadn't mentioned the wrench then, but after Agnes found it and his prints were identified, he added the detail that he had just picked up the wrench when he tripped over it going up the stairs to the apartment, realized he was still holding it when he fled, and on an impulse heaved it beyond the compost pile into the weeds.

The story was implausible enough to be true. It might have been Amos Cadbury who picked up that wrench when he went up those stairs later, and he might have done the same thing Luke had—gotten rid of it, or thought he had—but Cadbury at least had reported finding the body. Putting Luke on trial was going to be almost like putting Cadbury in the dock. Agnes wondered if she was unconsciously operating under one of those two constraints when she began to think of extenuating circumstances helpful to Luke Flanagan.

Forget about the wrench. Think of that apartment, which at the moment of the crime had been the bachelor pad of Gregory Packer. The lab had gone through the place and found only a couple of Packer's prints.

"You check those dishes?"

"We checked those dishes."

There wasn't a dirty dish in evidence. If they had been washed, someone had to stack them in the cupboards, and how are you going to stack dishes without leaving prints on them? The thumb of one of those rubber gloves in the kitchen sink seemed to be at someone's nose, the fingers waggling at her. Someone had wiped that place clean as a whistle. Agnes could imagine a lawyer making the case that the nature of Luke's prints on the wrench was compatible with his having picked it up, as he said, but not with his having used it as a weapon. So maybe they weren't just showing deference to a local icon. Robertson might have been bought and paid for, but Keegan and Cy Horvath weren't. If that wrench and some mouthing off Luke Flanagan had done about Gregory Packer were their case, they were as likely to lose it as win it. Where did that put them?

Cy had been trained by Keegan, and she had been trained by Cy, so she knew that an investigation did not consist of making up stories about what might have happened. A little logical jump or two was okay, but the jump had to be from fact to fact. On her way out to the Flanagan house, to take one more good look at the garage apartment, Agnes found herself dwelling on the presence of Marco Pianone at the wake for Gregory Packer.

"Why was he there?" she asked Cy.

"He came with that woman."

"Who is she?"

"Sylvia Beach. She worked for Wally Flanagan before he disappeared."

"What's that got to do with Packer?"

"Showing sympathy with the Flanagans?" He said it as if he dared her to believe it.

Maybe if she had come alone you could believe that, but if she had come alone who would have given her two thoughts? It was showing up with Marco Pianone that made her noticeable.

"Is Marco your brother?" she asked Peanuts.

He looked at her with his little pig eyes. She didn't get his answer the first time and asked him to repeat it.

"Cousin!"

"What's he do?"

"Ask him." He turned and waddled away.

Marco, she learned, managed a large portion of the Pianone gambling casinos, on land and water, all perfectly legal. Before long the Pianones would be as legitimate as the Looneys had become, what was left of them. Luke Flanagan's nephew Frank, the one who took over the cement business when Luke's son decided on high finance, was a Looney. You couldn't get any straighter than Frank Looney. Agnes had talked with him when they revived the investigation into Wallace Flanagan after the discovery of his body.

"Why here?" she had asked Frank.

"What do you mean?"

"Why would the body be jammed into a cement mixer owned by his father? It looks like a message."

Frank just shook his head, saying how awful it was.

She had heard about Luke Flanagan reading the riot act to Robertson because the Pianones had expressed interest in investing in Flanagan Concrete. Now she asked Frank if that was true.

"It's not going to happen."

"Were they interested?"

"We talked, sure, but nothing came of it."

"Who is we?"

"They came to me."

"Who's they?"

"Marco Pianone."

Maybe if you knew enough, everything in the universe was connected with everything else, all pieces of a huge puzzle that only seemed unrelated. She could jump from one fact about Marco to another, but where did she jump from there?

At the Flanagan house, she pulled into the driveway and parked. A four-bay garage! Well, it went with the house, which looked like a mansion to Agnes. She got out of the car. The site was still ribboned off, and Wimple was on duty, her hips fighting with her uniform skirt for supremacy. She was smiling and moving about. Agnes saw the cord of the earphones crawling up Wimple's bosom. Even with an iPod this was pretty boring duty. Wimple came toward her, removing the plugs from her ears. "Am I relieved?"

"To see me?"

Wimple's shoulders slumped. "Oh well, only a couple hours left in my shift."

"Anyone been nosing around?"

"Only some woman and Tuttle, the lawyer."

"Did you get her name?"

"I recognized Tuttle."

"What did he want?"

"Just wanted to go into the garage."

"What for?"

"The garage isn't part of the site."

"How long were they here?"

Wimple shrugged, her badge lifting and falling. "Fifteen minutes, maybe half an hour."

A side door of the house opened, and Luke Flanagan and Maud Lynn emerged. Agnes went up to them. They were both smiling like a couple of kids. Geez. Melissa Flanagan was standing in the still-open door, and Luke called to her to open the garage door. "If you don't mind, we have to bail out, Agnes. I'm taking Maud to the airport."

They went into the garage, car doors slammed, and soon he was backing out. It was a little tight, with her patrol car there, but he made it. Melissa waved good-bye.

"Leave the garage door open, will you?" Agnes asked.

Inside the garage, Agnes looked around, wondering what Tuttle and the unnamed woman had been doing here. She used her flashlight at first, before finding the lights. Only one car was parked here now, in the fourth bay, farthest from the house. There was a workbench with all kinds of tools. Had the wrench come from here? If so, whoever had used it would have had to enter the garage to get it. The sound the garage door made going up should have let Greg Packer know he had company.

"I'm going up," she told Wimple when she came out.

"Want me to shut that door?"

"Leave it up for now."

Agnes lifted the yellow tape and went around to the back of the garage. There was a tag on the door. That was another thing: There had been no prints on the handle of this door, nor on the one upstairs. Both Packer and whoever killed him might have been ghosts.

She turned on the stair light and mounted slowly, studying each step for anything that might have been overlooked. Nothing. Then she was in the apartment. She went through it systematically, room by room. In the bedroom, the bed was made, neat and tight. Were bachelors such good housekeepers? In the kitchen, she looked at the sink—the gloves were at the lab, of course, not that they had told them anything—and then once more at the neat stacks of dishes in the cupboard. She pushed open the door to the pantry, realizing that she had previously written it off as unimportant. She turned on the light and went in. The main smell was faint: coffee. The shelves held some canned goods. It was when she turned to leave that her shoe caught, and she looked down.

She stepped out of the pantry and knelt in the doorway, studying the floor. There seemed to be a rectangular inset in the floor, like the piece of a puzzle that just fit. Did it lift? There seemed nothing to catch hold of. Then she noticed the button attached to the bottom of one of the shelves. She pressed it.

The inset panel gave a little jerk and then began slowly to lift. Agnes was outside the pantry now, with her flashlight on, watching the panel rise to a right angle with the floor. When she trained her light on the opening, she saw aluminum. The quiet whirring sound clicked on, and then the aluminum moved. Agnes watched it drop and unfold and become a ladder to the garage below.

Going down it was like climbing a rope in reverse because the sections of the ladder were not rigidly linked. She found herself standing to the right of the workbench. She looked for and found the twin of the button in the pantry. When she pressed it, the ladder folded into itself and lifted. When it was stored, the panel in the ceiling of the garage lifted into place.

"I thought you went upstairs," Wimple said when she came out of the garage.

Agnes just hurried past Wimple to her car and the radio. Wait until Cy heard about that ladder.

18

It was the doorman, Ferret, who had put her onto the rental in her old building. Sandra had stopped to greet him when she was out for her run, and he seemed genuinely glad to see her after so many years. Where was she staying? The Whitehall. That was where he sent her the notice of the apartment available for two months. Furnished, of course. Did she want to return to the building she had left long ago with such hopes of a new life? It turned out she did.

She was closer to her father's retirement home than she had ever been, and she began to drop by every other day or so, not that he gave a damn. Sandra was his wayward daughter, the one who had let him down. Her sister had been twenty years older and was now gone to God. Her father had been alone so long that Sandra wondered if he even remembered living with his family. She had rescued him from the pits so far as retirement homes went, a one-story L-shaped building that smelled of urine. The occupants had to sit in the hall outside their rooms most of the day, so they could be watched, apparently. None of the staff spoke Polish.

Her father had sat with his mouth and his fly open, staring across the narrow corridor in which he sat. He needed a shave; he needed a bath. When she rolled him out of there she expected him to cast blessings left and right, like Salieri in the film.

So she set him up in the high-rise retirement home run by the Franciscans. There was a chapel right in the building and a chaplain always on duty. Throughout all this, her father was passive, registering what was happening, not commenting. When she got him settled in his apartment, nice view both north and east, there was an awkward moment as daughter faced father.

"Isn't this better, Dad?"

"I don't know anyone here."

"You will."

"How about you?"

"I'll be back." She put a hand on his arm. She would have liked to lean over and kiss the hairless head, to do something to erase the long years when she hadn't even thought of him, let alone seen him. "I'll be back."

"What if I want a drink?"

"There's beer in the refrigerator."

How long had it been since he'd even had a beer? The place from which she had sprung him had boasted its smoke-free and alcohol-free status. She had put a six-pack in the fridge. That became the excuse for her visits, to make sure he had beer in his refrigerator. He liked the place, particularly the shower. He seemed always to be getting out of it when she visited, going naked to his clothes, using the wheelchair as a support. What would the world be like if everyone went around nude? Even her father improved when he was dressed.

He had no curiosity about where she had been all these years, which was fine with Sandra. He lived in the present, and that was that. If he had had memories, he had discarded them all. Life was today's game, what was on the menu, and, lately, the friends he had made who took him up the street to a bar.

Luke Flanagan! She recognized him from the wake, where he'd sat in the front row of folding chairs with the woman that was with him now.

"We're lifers, too," Maud said.

They cracked one another up, Luke and Maud. Her father just followed their banter as if it were an interruption. What would Luke think if he knew she was the woman his son had planned to run away with to California?

It was Tuttle who told her the name of the woman Wally had run off with. Sylvia Beach.

"How did you find that out?"

He adjusted his tweed hat. "The police are cooperating with me."

Had she ever had any illusions about Tuttle? No, doubts and hopes, but no illusions.

"She's living in the same building you are."

"She is?"

Tuttle nodded. Any comment he might have made would have been the wrong one; seeming to sense that, he remained silent.

"Where did they go?"

"I'm still working on that."

What did it matter? She might have asked him to send her his bill—he had done what she asked him to do—but she was curious to learn where Wally had gone. Curious? That made it sound like a neutral piece of information, one that didn't tear her apart when she thought about it. Since returning to Chicago, the thought of herself waiting in vain in San Diego for Wally to join her filled her with rage all over again. Her life there had evolved; there had been Greg, and there had been Oxnard and all the healing years, or so they had seemed. But in memory she was right back there in San Diego, a dum-dum waiting for the man who said they would begin a new life together. Tuttle's information removed once and for all the speculation that something had happened to Wally, some injury, something, that prevented him from letting her know why he wasn't coming. Yes, she did want to know where he had gone with Sylvia Beach.

"A bimbo," Ferret whispered when she asked about the woman with the blond crew cut.

"Is her name Sylvia Beach?"

"That isn't the name she's using."

How often do you see people who live in the same building you do? The first time she saw Sylvia, alerted by Ferret, Sandra was in her running costume—dark glasses, the bill of her baseball cap curved over her face—so she stood as if recovering from her run, looking at the other woman. She had been at Greg's wake! The suggestion of a connection with her former husband as well as with Wally was too much. Sandra approached the woman. "Hi. I'm Sandy."

"Hello."

"You live here, too, don't you?"

"I just moved in."

"I lived here years and years ago. Now I'm back."

The conversation didn't go anywhere—how could it?—but it gave Sandra a chance to study the woman who had lured Wally from her. Had she and this woman been competitors back then, auditioning for the role? Hating a stranger was a new experience.

"Hasta la vista," she said and turned to the elevator.

"Ciao."

Later that day, Ferret told her that the bimbo had been asking about her.

"Don't call her that."

"What did you call her?"

"Sylvia Beach."

"Okay. She wanted to know all about you. First time she ever talked to me."

The next time they ran into one another, Sandra had the sense that it wasn't an accident. Sylvia was sitting in the lobby when Sandra came in from her run, and she got up and stopped her on the way to the elevator.

"What a day to be running," Sylvia said.

"Did you ever try it?"

"With every kind of exercise machine right here in the building?"

"I got the habit in California."

"California."

"It's a long story."

"Most stories are."

They ought to have lunch sometime, or a drink. Sandra said that would be nice. Sylvia telephoned later that day, asking if she was free.

"Where should we go?"

"How about my place?"

"Better."

Ferret's description of Sylvia had not prepared Sandra for the apartment. It was wonderful, the furniture, the pictures, the appointments. She had expected an illicit bower, but Sylvia's apartment was more tasteful than the one Sandra occupied. California provided the opening gambit, and Sandra told her all about her life in Oxnard.

"A financial advisor!"

"It's a living."

"I knew a financial advisor."

"I hope you have one."

"Let's say I had one."

Sylvia couldn't believe that anyone from California would want to move to Chicago.

"I had one earthquake too many."

"We have tornadoes."

Getting to know Sylvia made it difficult to hate her. It was insane to think that sooner or later they would be able to talk about Wally. Sandra would give anything to know what had gone wrong with the plans she and Wally had made. She just could not believe that he had been deceiving her. It would have helped to think of Sylvia as a bimbo, the dyed crew cut and flamboyant makeup certainly suggested that, but they seemed a disguise rather than what she really was.

"I came here from Minnesota," Sylvia said, the second time they got together, for lunch in a restaurant on the Magnificent Mile.

"Minnesota!"

"I know, I know. Way up in the North Woods in a town you've never heard of."

"International Falls?"

"How in the world did you know of it?"

"It's mentioned in weather reports. The coldest spot in the country."

"We were south of there. Garrison."

"We?"

"My financial advisor and I."

"Your husband was a financial advisor?"

"He had been. He had made a pile and only wanted to fish and read and look out at the lake."

"Sounds nice."

"If you like to fish and read and look out at lakes."

"How could you get tired of something like that?"

Ah, but what would life in California with Wally have been like if he had joined her? Like her father, they would have tried to exist only in the present. Just the thought of being together, untrammeled by the past, had seemed attraction enough, but obviously that could get boring, as Sylvia's remark suggested.

"Oh, he got tired of it."

"And then?"

Sylvia sipped her daiquiri. "He left me."

"Oh."

"So I came back here."

"Back?"

"It's a long story."

When Sandra thought of what had happened to Wally, her attitude toward Sylvia altered once again.

"Be careful," Tuttle told her when she mentioned that she had come to know Sylvia Beach.

"Of what?"

"What do you know of the Pianones?"

"One of them is her guy, isn't he? Marco?"

"That's why I said be careful. Half the unsolved murders in Fox River are ascribed to the Pianones. Rightly or wrongly," he added. "Maybe it's just the name of the file they put cases in they can't solve."

"Like Wally Flanagan."

"That was a twist. A cement mixer."

Knowledge is supposed to be power, but the more she learned, the less Sandra knew what to do with it. Sylvia was being kept by a Pianone. Had Wally just been in the way and been taken care of in the usual family manner? It was clear to Sandra that the Fox River police would not want to pursue that possibility.

The following morning, as she was going through the lobby, about to start her run, a very large man in plainclothes and a black woman in uniform stopped her.

"Sandra Bochenski?" the woman asked.

"You're Horvath," Sandra said to the big guy. "We've talked."

"This is Officer Lamb. Agnes. We want to talk some more."

"Sure."

Agnes Lamb said, "We're investigating the murder of your husband."

"My husband!"

"Gregory Packer."

Over by his pulpit, Ferret was trying not to make his eavesdropping obvious.

"My former husband."

"We'd like you to come with us."

"Why? We can talk right here."

Agnes Lamb took a sheet from the envelope she had been carrying. It was a warrant for the arrest of Sandra Bochenski.

The arrest of Sandra Bochenski on suspicion of murdering her former husband, Gregory Packer, turned everyone into a legal expert, even Tuttle. Phil Keegan passed on to Father Dowling the tantrum the little lawyer had thrown before the questioning began. How could they suspect his client when they had the killer in custody?

"Out on bail, of course," Tuttle had thundered. "What's a little manslaughter if you're rich and powerful?"

"Will you release Luke Flanagan, Phil?" Father Dowling asked.

"There's a division of opinion. Robertson is for. Jacuzzi is against and threatens to resign and make a public statement if Luke is let off."

"The famous wrench."

"Exactly. But Tuttle couldn't keep quiet about the ladder entrance to the garage apartment that Agnes discovered. He told Mervel that Sandra and Wally spent time in the apartment, entering and exiting by the ladder."

"And jeopardized his client? No wonder Tuttle is angered by the arrest."

Presumably, the case against Sandra Bochenski would seek motivation in her failed marriage to Gregory Packer. She had fled when he became abusive and resumed her life in Oxnard under her maiden name. He had divorced her, charging desertion, but his subsequent record did not suggest an injured party.

"She seems to have returned to Fox River when she learned that Packer was here."

"Seeking revenge for long-ago injuries?"

"She hired Tuttle to find out where Wally Flanagan was during his unaccounted-for years. It seems that she and Wally had an affair before she went to California. She expected him to meet her there."

"And he didn't."

"Instead she got Greg Packer, Wally's boyhood friend."

That meeting could hardly have been an accident. But who made it happen?

"Cy thinks that Wally might actually have told Greg about Sandra Bochenski, that she was pretty well off, thanks to his financial advice."

"And dispatched him as his substitute."

"He wouldn't have had to put it so baldly. The simple facts would have made her an attractive target for Greg. He had been out of the navy for a time and must have been looking for another meal ticket."

"Another?"

"You get three squares in the navy."

If Phil's account of all this seemed lurid, Mervel rose to new heights of uncontrolled prose. From multiple sources, he put together a detailed and tendentious narrative, filled with drama, betrayals, lust, and greed. Wally Flanagan was the spoiled little rich boy whose father had bankrolled him as a financial advisor, thus turning this predator loose on unsuspecting young ladies who had the great misfortune to work with or for him. That this wanton was also a married man only added to his turpitude. Mervel became a veritable poet of marital fidelity in his account. The idea that a young man, with every advantage in the world, with a lovely wife, should embark on such a Don Giovanni campaign, preying on sweet young things who came to Chicago to get their start and no doubt to meet an honest man as well—this would have left Mervel wordless if words were not his stock-in-trade. He was shameless in providing a dramatic scenario for the affair between Wally and Sandra. Mervel asked his readers to imagine the confusion, the sorrow, the anger with which Sandra realized that she had been abandoned in California the way Melissa had been in Fox River. The account came down out of the clouds when Mervel came to the discovery of Wally's body, the old local caution about the Pianones exhibiting itself, but the reporter could not resist a speculative wonder at the fact that Wally had ended up in one of his father's cement mixers.

"We'll have to keep Luke away from wrenches and other blunt instruments, Roger."

"Poor Melissa."

"At least he didn't bring up their reunion at the senior center here."

"Good Lord."

There was a diagram of the Flanagan garage, with an inset showing the descending ladder that provided an alternative entry and exit to the apartment above. It was up this ladder that Wally took his paramours, sinning within spitting distance of his father's home.

Tuttle tried to file a libel suit against Mervel and the *Fox River*

Tribune but got nowhere. The freedom of the free press had long since passed the quaint canons of decency that Tuttle improbably invoked.

"If national security secrets are fair game, how could the reputations of those who figured in Mervel's account provide grounds for libel?" This was Amos Cadbury's melancholy observation when he had himself driven to Father Dowling's noon Mass and accepted an invitation to lunch.

"Surely there is less of a case against Sandra Bochenski than there is against Luke Flanagan."

"Ah, Father Dowling, you are making the charming assumption that cases are still tried in the courts. That newspaper account could be the sum total of what will be done against either of them. Having been condemned in print and on film, what need is there to bother with a trial?"

"I wonder how Melissa is taking this?"

"You should talk to her, Father."

"Have you?"

Amos had talked to Luke as well as to Melissa, as friend, as lawyer. "Luke is tough, of course, but poor Melissa. I keep thinking of that wedding ring in my safe."

"Wedding ring?"

"The ring found on the hand of the body extracted from the cement mixer. It was the basis of identifying the body. Since neither Luke nor Melissa would take it, it ended up in my office safe."

As Father Dowling returned to his study from seeing Amos off, he heard voices in the kitchen. Curious, he continued down the hall and pushed open the door.

Marie sat at one end of the table, while at the other a bearded man was eating the sandwich she had made for him. The man rose when Father Dowling entered the kitchen.

"I'm sorry to interrupt."

He waited to see if Marie would say anything, and when she didn't he retreated to his study. Recent events weighed on him, not least because there seemed nothing he could do to lessen their burden on the Flanagans. He pulled the telephone to him and dialed the Flanagan number. What better time than the present to go see Melissa? But no one answered.

Fifteen minutes later, Marie looked in on him. "He's gone." He realized that she meant the bearded vagrant she had fed. "You don't mind, do you? I could have brought food to him on the back porch."

"Nonsense. He seemed a pleasant enough fellow." He paused. "A sort of Franciscan look."

Marie's mouth became a line, and she glared at him. Then she went back to her kitchen, slamming the door behind her.

20

Luke wasn't all that eager to come back to his apartment, preferring to stay in Fox River with his daughter-in-law, and Maud knew the reason was Boleslaw Bochenski. It had been just a lark the first time they wheeled the old guy down to their bar and made sure he had a couple of boilermakers; it was as if they were young and Boleslaw was old, although Luke wasn't sure that the wheelchair was necessary.

"He just likes to be pushed around," Luke asserted.

"He's a man."

Luke hadn't liked the way Boleslaw whined about how his daughter neglected him. If she ever had in the past, she was making up for it now, so they got to know Sandra, too, she and Luke. That, of course, was the problem. Luke had treated Boleslaw the way he had probably treated employees, and now to find that Sandra Bochenski had had an affair with his dead son, that they had planned to run away together, hit him hard. The fact that his son had run off with another woman, thus stranding Sandra as well as Melissa, didn't register with Luke. Before those stories appeared in the Fox River paper, Maud would have said Luke liked Sandra, admired her. Unlike her father, she had independence. She clearly wasn't dependent on anyone else.

"Anyone but Tuttle," he said. "I would have warned her if she had asked me about Fox River lawyers. Tuttle is a joke. I would have set her up with Amos Cadbury."

That would have been a pair. Maud half expected that Cadbury would have the family crest embossed on the door of the car in which he was driven around. Aristocratic, deferential, aloof, although he always talked to Maud as if they shared a secret. It turned out that Luke had told the lawyer that if he ever got married again, Maud would be the girl. Girl! Well, Luke hadn't exactly asked, so she hadn't answered, but that seemed another idea that was a casualty of these awful revelations about Luke's family. The fact that his son had used the garage apartment for a rendezvous, taking Sandra there, might have been sufficient to keep him away from the apartment here for which he had paid through the nose. The fact was that Maud was lonely.

She had returned from her trip to Kentucky to visit her son the monk. A few days was all of it she could take. Jimmy—she could never think of him as Brother Peter—accepted her visits as if he were doing penance. He had put her and the world behind him, but, of course, it was his duty to honor his mother. Maud didn't want to be honored, not in that way. She didn't know what she expected from Jimmy, but it wasn't his dutiful presence when he spent time with her in the guesthouse.

One day they had taken a long walk, along a road that went through the monastery woods to the hermitage that, he said, was famous because Thomas Merton had spent so much time there. Merton had been a monk at Gethsemani, and Jimmy seemed to have ambiguous thoughts about him. Not that he would criticize anyone. What kind of conversation could you have with someone who was determined to see only good in other people? Another guest, the one with the beard, was already at the hermitage, sitting on the front porch, looking off into the hills in the distance. The man got up as they approached, ready to leave the hermitage to them, but Jimmy insisted they didn't want to disturb him.

"How long's he been here?" Maud asked when they started back.

Jimmy didn't know. What is time when all your thoughts are on eternity? She told Jimmy about Luke Flanagan, and he listened politely, but he might have been hearing the music of the spheres.

The first time Maud saw Boleslaw's daughter after she was taken in for questioning and the news about her and young Flanagan broke, she just went up to her and put her arms around her, no need to say anything.

There were tears in Sandra's eyes. "I didn't do it."

"Of course you didn't."

"Of course? Oh, I could have. There were times when I would have found it easy. He needed punishment, but I didn't want to be the one administering it."

"We all need punishment." She might have been expressing Jimmy's thoughts.

"I think he killed Wally Flanagan."

"No."

Her story rivaled the one that had appeared in the paper. It made soap operas seem hard realism. Maud would never have dreamed when she met Luke and they became friendly that she would find him and his family involved in all these gothic horrors. The only ghost she had in her own closet was a son who was a Trappist monk.

"What will happen next?" Maud asked Sandra.

"To me? My lawyer doesn't think they'll dare to bring charges." She had been taken in for questioning, held for a while, and then released. She wore dark glasses now, even indoors, no doubt fearful that she would be recognized. She said that when this was over she might go back to California.

"I thought you took an apartment."

"Just a sublet for a few months. To be near Dad."

Did Boleslaw know what she was going through? When he wasn't watching sports on television or drinking beer, or both, he just sat slumped in his wheelchair, lost in thought. Jimmy might have imagined that he was meditating on his life, thinking long thoughts about time and eternity, preparing to meet his God. Maud didn't think it was uncharitable not to attribute that to Boleslaw. When he did speak, it was about some ache or pain or something else that annoyed him.

"Where've you been?" he groused when Sandra showed up after her ordeal in Fox River.

Sandra seemed happy that he didn't know. "Maud, why don't we go up the street and buy Dad a beer."

"I was just going to suggest the same thing."

It was the kind of lie Jimmy might have approved of.

21

As soon as the alternative entrance and exit to the Flanagan garage apartment became known, Amos Cadbury, on behalf of his client, demanded an inspection of all the tools arrayed above and around the workbench in the garage, a move that Tuttle grudgingly appreciated.

"To free Mr. Flanagan of suspicion of wrongdoing is, of course, easily done, but my client insists that the outrageous crime committed in the garage apartment of his home be speedily solved," Amos asserted.

Cadbury didn't exactly accuse Jacuzzi and Robertson of idiocy; nor did he criticize the thus far inconclusive efforts of Captain Keegan's detective division. He spoke from such lofty high ground that those judgments were remote inferences from what he said. Tuttle might have tried the same tack but knew that he would sound ridiculous. His client, bless her soul, had been turned into a painted woman, a ruthless housebreaker, by the traitor Mervel.

"The public has a right to know, Tuttle," Mervel said unctuously.

"Then they should know you were drunk when you wrote it."

"Sticks and stones, Tuttle. Sticks and stones."

Well, the pressroom in the courthouse did have the culture of an elementary school playground. Ninian slept on the Naugahyde couch; Bea Hyverson, of the *PennySaver*, a shopping guide left gratis in every local mailbox, knitted away in a corner while surveying the room over the rims of her glasses. Mervel himself had brought up an old file from his hard drive, the one labeled NOVEL, and was folding recent events into the narrative.

Tuttle sipped the coffee he had let trickle into a Styrofoam cup and spit it back. "Who made this coffee?"

"Coffee?" Bea cried. "Don't drink that stuff."

Tuttle got out of there and went upstairs to Keegan's office. "Any results from those other tools, Captain?"

"They're in the lab."

"Good."

"I'm glad you approve."

Tuttle left the office and went to the railing that gave him a bird's-eye view of the black-and-white tile floor four flights below. A circular staircase wound down toward it, and an open elevator of ancient vintage dropped like a plumb line, its cable greasy and twisted. Abandon all hope ye who enter here. Tuttle took the stairs. As he descended, he had the feeling that he was winding up the string of recent events into a ball. Maybe when he got to the ground floor they would make some sense.

The trouble with that ladder that led from the main garage to the pantry in the apartment above was that you had to know it was there in order to use it. Luke Flanagan said he had completely forgotten it and, when he remembered, couldn't believe the thing still worked. It had been his son's idea, a boy's whim catered to in the forgotten past. Melissa had known nothing of it. Sandra Bochenski had shown it to Tuttle, which meant two things: She had known it was there, and she didn't see knowledge of it as any threat to her. No one else seemed to know of the trapdoor and collapsible ladder.

Hazel put away the crossword when he got to the office, glaring at him as if she had found him goofing off, rather than the reverse. Then again, what else did she have to do?

"Has your client skipped town yet?"

"She won't leave until I give the word. I want her name cleared."

Hazel ducked her head and looked at him.

"No calls," he said and went into the inner office. He seemed to be shutting out her derisive laughter when he closed the door.

Sandra Bochenski was torn between the desire to escape to California and concern for her father, Boleslaw. How could Tuttle not respond to that touching concern for her parent? He himself had an almost Oriental devotion to his parents, especially to his father, whose encouragement and support had survived Tuttle's checkered and prolonged progress through law school.

Remembering Cadbury's lofty statement, Tuttle realized that the only thing that would clear his client's name was to identify the killer of Gregory Packer. Of course, the police did not seriously think that Sandra had killed the man.

"Sure I could have. There were times when killing him would have been a form of self-defense," she said to Tuttle.

"Our conversations are confidential. Don't talk like that to anyone else."

"I already have."

"Who?"

"Sylvia."

Sylvia was the bimbo stashed in the same building by Marco Pianone.

"How long has she been hooked up with Pianone?"

"You want me to ask her?"

"No!"

"She was really surprised when she read that Greg had been my husband."

"Did she know him?"

"She said Wally Flanagan talked about him. They had a lot of time to talk up there in the North Woods. He loved it, but she was cabin-crazy most of the time."

"How long?"

"Years."

"What did he do?"

"Fish, read, go for long walks."

There are those for whom such a schedule would seem heaven on earth, but Tuttle was not among them. He could sympathize with Sylvia Beach.

"She ever say why he went off with her rather than go to California to be with you?"

"Blackmail."

"Blackmail?"

"She found out about our plan. Her suspicions were aroused when he told her he wanted to arrange her portfolio so her worries would be over. What worries? The future. It sounded like the payoff for their affair. So she followed him, saw us together, and then confronted him, threatening to blow the whistle. Her alternative was that they do what Wally and I planned to do. That's how she got him. He had no choice."

"You don't sound bitter." It was an odd thought, the two of them talking about the guy they had both been seeing, a married man.

"He deserted her."

"Come on."

"One day, she came back from town—there was a bar there she liked and Wally didn't—and he was gone. No note, nothing. Just gone. He might have done that to me."

"She have any idea how he ended up dead in Fox River?"

"I'll ask her."

"Don't."

Reviewing this conversation in his inner office, feet on the desk, tweed hat pulled over his eyes, Tuttle didn't like the way the Pianones kept coming to mind. Wally's body in the cement mixer had the Pianone touch, and maybe so did the murder of Gregory Packer. It turned out that he had put the touch on Sylvia, too, wanting backing for a driving range in Barrington— but Melissa Flanagan had already agreed to finance that project. If Marco thought some guy was trying to put the squeeze on Sylvia . . .

These were not thoughts to pursue, not even in the privacy of his own mind. They would occur to Cy Horvath sooner or later, he supposed. From what Peanuts told him, Tuttle knew that Horvath knew at least as much as he did. But how willing was Horvath to pursue the Pianone connection, if there was one?

22

When Greta came into his office, carefully shutting the door behind her, she was holding a folded piece of paper in such a way that Amos Cadbury's eyes were drawn to it.

"He asked me to give you this. Unread." She seemed to be pleading for understanding. "He was so polite. I thought he wanted a handout, but when I opened my purse, he just shook his head."

"A handout?"

Amos had taken the note. Greta stood waiting as he read it. He read it twice and then turned his chair toward the window. What a dreadful joke. He was astonished that Greta had allowed herself to be used in this way. He turned back to her.

"Describe him."

Her description of the man made it even more incredible that she had been taken in. Still, she had offered him money, so her first reaction had been sensible.

"Will you see him, Mr. Cadbury?"

Greta seemed to have become the vagrant's advocate, but it was curiosity and controlled anger that prompted Amos to ask her to show the man in.

She hurried across the room, opened the door to the outer office, and stood in it, urging someone forward. She stepped aside, and a bearded middle-aged man entered and approached the desk.

"Good afternoon, Mr. Cadbury."

Was it the suggestion of the note, its preposterous claim, or this office in which years ago he had presided over the arrangements Luke had made with his son that gave him pause? Amos rose behind the desk and studied his visitor. He still held the note in his hand. He flourished it.

"Why have you come to me?"

"You're the family lawyer."

It was information anyone could have gathered from recent newspaper stories. The visitor looked around. "It was here that my father made me a rich man before my time."

Amos sat. "Go on."

The description of that event, of the discussions that had led up to it, of Amos's reluctance to preside over the premature inheritance, was uncannily accurate. Amos studied the man as he spoke, and against all reason, he began to see in this bearded fellow some resemblance to young Wally Flanagan.

"Wally Flanagan is dead, sir."

"I will not quote Mark Twain."

"Mrs. Flanagan identified the body."

"How?"

"By his wedding ring."

"May I sit?"

"What is the point of this farce?"

He held up a ringless left hand. "I can't imagine how my ring could have been found on a corpse."

Amos, certain the man was dropping the charade, gave him a

clinical description of the body, the body parts, that had been found in one of the Flanagan cement mixers.

"One of my father's?"

"In a Flanagan cement mixer," Amos repeated.

"You said body parts."

"The ring convinced her."

"I had stopped wearing it. For obvious reasons. I must have left it behind when I left Garrison. Yes, of course I did. In the sense that I had forgotten it. What happened to the ring?"

"Why do you ask?"

"Because I could describe it."

"Wedding rings are pretty much alike."

"There were inscriptions."

"Were there?"

"Our names and the date of the wedding."

Amos restrained himself from congratulating the man on his good guess.

"There was another inscription, too. Inside. It was Melissa's idea. 'Until death do us part.'"

"And that is what happened when Wallace Flanagan's body was found."

The man breathed deeply. "Of course you're skeptical. I expected that. I would think less of you if you weren't. But I have to convince you first. Otherwise, I will simply fade away."

There were intonations as the man spoke that were reminiscent of Luke. The facial hair was like a mask over the lower face, although the fellow had the same wide mouth as Luke. It was the eyes Amos found most unnerving.

"How can I convince you?"

"That you are a dead man? What is the point of all this?"

"I wanted to be of help to my father. I heard that he was suspected of killing a man. Gregory Packer."

"I suppose you knew Packer."

"We were kids together. We were classmates at St. Hilary's. Neither of us turned out very well."

"And now you're both dead."

It occurred to Amos that by allowing this preposterous conversation to go on, he was seemingly giving credence to the man's claim.

"He was best man at our wedding. Much to my father's displeasure."

"You have done a lot of research."

"In the smithy of my soul."

"Where have you come from?"

"Gethsemani. A Trappist monastery in Kentucky."

"You're a monk?"

"A penitent. They let me stay on, no questions asked. I had decided to remain dead, dead to all those I had betrayed, and spend my days trying to get right with God."

This was disarming, as it was no doubt intended to be. "What is it you really want?"

He looked beyond Amos. He spoke softly. "Forgiveness."

"You should see a priest."

"I have been living with monks. Confession is surprisingly easy, but it is hard to believe that one can be forgiven."

Amos wanted to tell the man that forgiveness for what he was attempting would be difficult to achieve.

"I have often prayed for my godmother."

Amos sat upright. "Did you?"

"Mrs. Cadbury. Aunt Helen."

Amos had wavered when the man described the inscriptions on the wedding band, and he had been unsettled by all the man seemed to know, but this mention of his departed wife undid him. He put his hands on the desk and leaned toward his visitor and, against his will, saw that he was Wally Flanagan.

From that point on, the conversation was very different from what it had been. Amos felt the layers of his skepticism melt away, but with the realization that, incredible as it was, he was talking to Wallace Flanagan, a host of other emotions came. The man had deserted his wife; he had been a womanizer, even betraying his mistresses; he had lived in seclusion and allowed his loved ones to imagine what they would of his whereabouts. Had he arranged for a body to be identified as his own?

"I have been weak and deceptive, but that would have been ghoulish. Sacrilegious."

"So how do you explain it?"

"I can't. I told you I left my ring behind in Garrison. Not by design. I hadn't worn it for years. It would have been in a dresser drawer. She must have found it."

"She?"

"Sylvia. We had gone off together and settled in a lake place in northern Minnesota. She came to hate the solitude. I urged her to go, but she refused. She was determined to make life such a hell for me there that we would leave together. When I left, I left alone."

It was some time later that he heard the startling news that his dead body had been discovered in Fox River.

"It is a strange experience to hear that one is dead. My first thought was that I was finally free of the past. Eventually, I realized that I could never be free of it. I ended up in that monastery in Kentucky."

Greta buzzed and asked if there was anything he wanted her to do before she left for the day. He realized he had spent the better part of two hours with his client, for that was the status Wally Flanagan once more had. However long the list of his wrongdoings, though, there seemed no indictable offense among them.

"So what shall I do?"

"There is a priest I want you to see. Father Dowling, the pastor at St. Hilary's."

"Will you tell him my story?"

"No. You are going to have to convince him who you are."

"Have I convinced you?"

For answer, Amos went to the wall safe, moving aside the portrait of his wife to get to it, and brought forth an envelope. He handed it to Wally Flanagan.

He read the inscription on the envelope; he opened it; he took out the ring and held it before his face. There were tears in his eyes when, with an effort, he put it on his finger. It was a ceremonial deed. At least in the eyes of Amos Cadbury, Wally Flanagan had returned.

23

It was odd how current events seemed always to point back to the disappearance of Wallace Flanagan. Now that who he had gone off with was known, and where, the plight of Sandra Bochenski seemed even more pathetic. Mervel put the main burden of young Flanagan's infidelity on her, but she had reaped none of the benefits, if that was the right word. It was Sylvia Beach who had fled with the faithless husband, improbably into the North Woods of Minnesota.

"Not all that improbable, Roger," Phil Keegan said. "The Flanagans always vacationed up in Wisconsin, near the Dells, Lake Delton, renting a cottage for the summer. It was young Flanagan's favorite place."

Roger Dowling knew the area and had been part of the traffic on I-90 and I-94, the two routes one traveled when going through the Dells, branching off at Tomah, one going west to La Crosse, the other continuing north to Eau Claire, both ending in Minnesota. It was the area in which he had been restored to health before being assigned to St. Hilary's in Fox River, the end of his presumed destiny for ecclesiastical advancement but, as it turned out, the true beginning of his priesthood. One man's exile is another's home, and Fox River had become home to him.

"Luke told me that when Wally said he didn't want to succeed his father in the cement business, one reason was that it seemed a life sentence. He wanted only enough security so that he could live the way they had at Lake Delton for the rest of his life."

"Yet he deserted Sylvia Beach, too, in the end."

"And ended his life in the cement business." Phil sipped his beer. He was not as complacent as he seemed. He had little more confidence in the case against Sandra Bochenski than he had in that against Luke Flanagan. "Cy went up to Garrison, Minnesota, and checked out Wally Flanagan's time there. He was considered a character locally. He went native, quit shaving, was a frequent visitor to the town library, carting home books to read in a lawn chair in front of his lake place. Or in front of the fireplace in winter."

"Sounds idyllic."

"If you're a monk. Of course, he had Sylvia, too."

"When did he leave there?"

Phil smiled. "Before Sylvia did."

Maud Lynn's son was a genuine monk, not that she showed the usual parental pride in a religious vocation in the family. Jimmy had visited Gethsemani to make a retreat when he was trying to decide what to do with his life. He never left the monastery, having found there what he was looking for.

"Life on the farm," Maud said. "Woods, silence, cattle. He looks after the bees. They make cheese, too."

Father Dowling knew. He had made a retreat there himself, during his troubled days on the Archdiocesan Marriage Court when he had been undone by all the insoluble cases, people seeking release from their promises when release could not be given.

For all Maud's alleged lack of sympathy with her son the monk, she loved to give detailed accounts of her stays in the guesthouse at Gethsemani, memories refreshed by her recent visit.

"Maybe that's where I belong," Luke said.

"They have a Flanagan already."

Father Dowling asked what she meant, and she explained.

"There are lots of Flanagans," Luke said.

"One too many."

"Maybe one too few."

Were they serious? They were constantly kidding each other, particularly about their impending nuptials, but that seemed to be all it was, kidding.

Marie Murkin wasn't too sure. "It would spring both of them from that retirement home. They could move back into the house."

"Or into the garage apartment."

Marie made a face. Her eyes lifted, and then she went to the window. "There he is."

Father Dowling looked out. On one of the benches, the vagrant Marie had fed the other day was comfortably settled, his arm on the back of the bench, looking toward the school.

"It's the risk you run when you feed them," Marie grumbled.

"Has he come back?"

"There he is."

"I mean for food."

It turned out that he hadn't asked for food the first time, Marie had just assumed he had come to the door for a handout. "I wonder if he came to see you."

"That would be a novelty. When they come to the back door, I assume they're your suitors."

She went off in a huff. Father Dowling continued to look out at the bearded man on the bench. When he decided to go out to him, he left by the front door.

"Welcome," he said, taking a seat beside the fellow.

He had startled the man, causing him to look directly at Father Dowling.

"We use the school as a center for retired folk now."

"Good idea."

"You might want to look into it."

"Am I eligible?"

"There are people your age there. Has it changed much?"

"Changed?"

"Introibo ad altare Dei."

Again the man looked directly at him, his expression difficult to read because of the beard. When he spoke, it was slowly, summoning the words from a distant past. *"Ad Deum qui laetificat iuventutem meam."*

Father Dowling nodded. "There are things one never forgets."

"Do you say Mass in Latin still?"

"Once a week. But without an altar boy."

He nodded, waiting for what Father Dowling might say next.

"Gregory Packer was an altar boy here in your time, wasn't he?"

"Yes."

"Have you heard what happened to him?"

"That's why I'm here."

"Risen from the dead."

"What shall I do?"

❧ Part Three ❧

The return of Wally Flanagan, apparently from the dead, could not simply be announced. Its effect on Melissa, on his father, and in various degrees on others had to be taken into account before it could be treated as an item of news for the general public. More immediately, Father Dowling would have to make known to Mrs. Murkin the identity of the man he had invited to occupy the guest room in the rectory.

"The guest room!"

"Isn't it ready?"

"Of course it's ready." Marie was finding it difficult to express her amazement in a whisper. Not even the Franciscans had gone this far. She looked beyond Father Dowling and said, still whispering, "Where is he?"

"In the study."

As if on cue, Wally Flanagan emerged. "Father, if it's any trouble, I can just go back to my motel."

"Marie, why don't you show our guest upstairs to his room."

"You're the boss. Come on." Marie began to mount the front stairway, then turned. "Do you have any luggage?"

"We'll pick that up later, Marie," Father Dowling said.

She turned and again started up much like the penitents who mount the Scala Sancta in Rome. Marie might not be going upstairs on her knees, but it was clear that she found the pastor's orders just slightly this side of the line of duty. In eloquent body language, she informed an indifferent world that if the pastor of St. Hilary's chose to lodge vagrants in the rectory, bearded nobodies from off the road, then she was resigned to being slain in her bed.

When she came down, she breezed past the open study door and into her kitchen. Father Dowling followed her. "Sit down, Marie."

"Yes, Father."

"You're probably wondering why I've asked Wally to stay here."

"It has crossed my mind." A double take. "Who?"

"You can't be any more surprised than I am."

"Did you say Wally?"

"You must have noticed the family resemblance."

"Wally Flanagan?" She mouthed the words, but no sound emerged.

"Exactly."

"Dear God in heaven! But he's dead."

"So we all thought."

A look of suspicion crept across Marie's face. "This is some kind of joke, isn't it?"

"Ah, then you did notice."

"Notice what?"

"His wedding ring. That, of course, was the basis of identifying a body as his."

"He's an impostor?"

"Not at all. Marie, I was sure you would recognize one of the old altar boys of the parish."

"They said a funeral Mass for him," Marie said.

"So they thought."

"But . . ." Words would not come; she looked at him suspiciously, then pleadingly, finally in total confusion. He sat across from her.

"You've taken this very well, Marie. Not that I'm surprised. I was counting on that. Imagine how this turn of events will strike Melissa Flanagan, Luke Flanagan, others. We are going to have to proceed with great caution and consideration."

It helped some, not much, when he likened the situation to the return of the prodigal son. That turned Marie's thoughts to the preparation of dinner. "I do have some lamb chops."

"Good. Good." He insisted that Marie join them at table.

But Wally Flanagan had become a vegetarian, and the lamb chops were left to Marie and Father Dowling. "I didn't make any big promise or anything, Father, but staying at the monastery, I got out of the habit of eating meat. It's surprising how little you miss it."

"Brother Peter's mother mentioned having seen you when she was visiting her son."

"She recognized me?"

"In logic classes, a distinction would be made. I see a stranger coming, the stranger is Wally, can I say I see Wally coming? She saw a bearded man named Flanagan."

"But it was you who made the connection?"

"If you hadn't remembered the Latin responses for the prayers at the foot of the altar, I don't know what I would have done next."

"That took me by surprise."

"Took *you* by surprise," Marie said. Her expression suggested that she was remembering the sins of his past life. "So why did you decide to rise from the dead?"

He had come upon a newspaper, an old one, one that Maud had left after her visit. The news had ceased to interest him, but he glanced at the paper, and that was how he became aware of events in Fox River. Reading of what had happened in the old family home, and that his father was suspected of murder, made it clear that remaining in monastic seclusion was self-indulgence.

"I had not been a good son to him." He said this slowly, then shook his head. "How inadequate that sounds. And then Melissa . . ."

Marie melted before this contrition, obviously heartfelt. "Imagine how delighted they will be," she cried.

"Once I got here, I began to doubt that. How many I've betrayed. So I have been vacillating. I have a habit of disappearing, and I thought maybe I should disappear again. I came here, intending to speak to Father Dowling, but you gave me something to eat, and I lost courage. When I was sitting on one of the benches, I heard a group of older folks from the school mention Melissa. Could it possibly be my Melissa? I wanted to catch at least a glimpse of her."

"And did you?"

"How unchanged she seems."

So the first hurdle, Marie Murkin, was cleared, and the question arose as to how to proceed. Father Dowling suggested having

Phil Keegan over, introducing their guest, and then playing it by ear.

Marie vetoed this.

"No, no. Cy Horvath. Nothing could surprise him."

"Cy Horvath?" Wally seemed doubtful.

"You were altar boys together," Marie said.

"I can imagine what he thinks of me."

"That is the least of your troubles." Marie was entering into the spirit of the thing. If she could play a role in orchestrating the return of Wally Flanagan, she was more than ready. "Father Dowling likened your return to that of the prodigal son. I doubt that you can expect universal rejoicing."

Marie had taken exactly the right tack. It was as a remorseful penitent that Wally Flanagan had returned, and he had few illusions as to the reception he could expect.

"Are you going to call Cy?" Marie asked.

Father Dowling rose. "I want to speak to Amos first."

Wally said, "I was going to suggest that. I've already seen him."

In the doorway, Father Dowling turned. "You did?"

Marie said, "I'll get these dishes off the table."

Wally offered to help.

"Just be careful. These are the good dishes."

2

Phil Keegan figured that if Amos Cadbury and Roger Dowling thought the man was Wally Flanagan, that was good enough for him. It wasn't good enough for Cy Horvath, and he didn't want to talk to the fellow at St. Hilary's, where he had been accepted as Wally Flanagan.

"Do you want him to come downtown, Cy?" Father Dowling asked.

"I'll pick him up." Cy paused. "In front of the church."

Driving out to St. Hilary's, Cy wondered if he was the only one who saw the real implications of this supposed return. Say it really was Wally, they might finally have the solution to the killing of Greg Packer. If nothing else, the man who had convinced Amos Cadbury and Roger Dowling had apparently made himself knowledgeable about the life of Wally Flanagan. So why wouldn't he know about the garage apartment, the alternative entry? Of course, anyone who read the papers knew of that trapdoor and ladder now, but who had known of it at the time Greg was killed? Sandra Bochenski, and that was only because Wally had shown it to her. Whoever this guy was, Cy had personal as well as professional reasons to want to talk to him.

The man had been sitting on the steps of the church and looked curiously at Cy's car as he pulled to the curb. Cy waited. The bearded man rose, looking like any other bum, and shuffled toward the car. He bent and looked in. Cy rolled down the window.

"Hello, Cyril. I expected the Batmobile." He opened the door and got in. "So you're still fighting crime."

Cy pulled away from the curb. His expression did not show the surprise he had felt at the guy's mention of his boyhood enthusiasm for Batman comics. "You like Chinese food?"

"I prefer Italian."

So they went to a Papa Vino's, Cy driving in silence, his passenger seemingly at ease.

"What do you make of the use they've put our old school to?"

Cy shrugged.

"I caught a glimpse of Melissa."

Cy turned and looked into the sad eyes of Wally Flanagan. Geez. First Greg Packer, now Wally.

"Where the hell have you been?"

"Hell is the word for it. Except for recently."

At the restaurant, Wally ordered a margherita pizza, just cheese and tomatoes, and Cy asked for spaghetti carbonara. "Wine?"

"Go ahead."

"I'm on duty."

"I'm on the wagon."

They settled for ice water. Eating seemed to be a way of putting off talking. Cy had imagined working the guy over, breaking his silly story, and here he was convinced he was having lunch with Wally Flanagan. He noticed the wedding ring.

"Amos gave it back to me."

"Amos?"

"He said neither my dad nor Melissa wanted it when they took it off that body. I wonder who it was."

"We'll find out."

"Can you do that?"

"We can do that."

"Good. Do you need proof, Cy?"

"It would only be a negative fact."

His heart wasn't in it, though. He was glad that neither Phil Keegan nor Agnes Lamb had been there to witness the collapse of his skepticism. Then he remembered his thoughts on the drive to St. Hilary's, and once more he was a cop. "When did you last see Greg Packer?"

"Greg? Years and years ago. Why did he come back?"

"He and Melissa were pretty close. Remember the apartment over the garage at your house?"

"Cy, I've read the papers."

"So you know Greg was staying there. Melissa was living in the house."

"What are you getting at?"

"Your old girlfriends came back to town, too. Sandra, Sylvia."

"What a shit I've been."

"That's been the consensus."

He accepted this agreement. Had he expected Cy to protest his self-description?

"And you've been questioning Sandra and my dad."

"Somebody killed Greg Packer."

"Neither of them could have done such a thing."

"Maybe you'll be called as a character witness."

"So what do I do now?"

"We'll go downtown, where you can dictate a statement, the whole sad story."

"Are you arresting me?"

"What would be the charge? Maybe your story can help us find out what happened to Greg Packer."

Tuttle was buying a package of gum in the little shop just off the courthouse rotunda when he saw Cy Horvath go by with a bearded man. Was Cy running in vagrants now? It was a slack time, but this seemed a stretch. Tuttle stepped out and watched them enter the elevator. From the large tiled area beneath the dome, he watched the cage go jerkily up to the top floor, where the detective division was housed. There was always the pressroom, where Tuttle could get a free cup of coffee, not yet toxic this early in the afternoon, or he might go up and see who Cy was hauling in. Not exactly the plight of Buridan's ass, but Tuttle hesitated. That was how Peanuts Pianone found him.

"Whatcha looking at?" Peanuts asked.

"Have you ever taken a good look at the painting in the dome?"

A personified Justice, blindfolded, held aloft a scale. She seemed to be floating in a sea of clouds.

"What saint is that?" Peanuts asked.

"Let's go upstairs."

"I can see it all right from here."

"Come on."

They took the stairway that wound around the interior of the great barrel that rose from the black-and-white-tiled first floor to the dome above.

They went to the pressroom, where they settled down with Styrofoam cups of not quite potable coffee. Ninian slept on the couch; Bea was frowning over a crossword puzzle; Mervel sat at his computer, eyes closed, fingers poised over the keyboard like Van Cliburn about to pounce. At work on his novel.

An irritating sound emanated from the inner pocket of Tuttle's seersucker jacket. He took out his cell phone, saw that it was Hazel on the line, and turned it off. Peanuts growled. Agnes Lamb had just passed swiftly by the open door. Tuttle's instinct told him that something was afoot. He got up and left the pressroom, strolling down the corridor. The door of Cy Horvath's office was closed. What is there about a closed door that excites curiosity? The closed door might be a metaphor of Tuttle's life. Peanuts had followed him.

"Find out what's going on," Tuttle ordered.

"Where?"

Tuttle nodded at Horvath's office. Peanuts went to the door and opened it. The bearded man sat across from Cy. There was a secretary with a shorthand typewriter clicking away. Agnes looked on. At the sight of her, Peanuts pulled the door closed.

Why would Cy be taking a statement from a vagrant? The

shorthand typist was Vivian McHugh, who had a crush on Tuttle, perhaps because he wore, summer and winter, an Irish tweed hat. Was he willing to wait until he could ask Vivian what was going on? Peanuts had gone off down the corridor, so Tuttle apparently had no choice. He returned to the pressroom, activated his phone, and called his office.

"Tuttle and Tuttle." Hazel's voice was brisk and efficient. For a moment Tuttle had the illusion that he was in contact with a flourishing law firm.

"You called."

"Is that you?" The only thing worse than Hazel's disdain was Hazel in a friendly mood. "Sandra Bochenski wants to see you, God knows why."

"Put me through."

"I'll give you the number."

She rattled it off, but Tuttle already had Sandra's number. Calling his client was the path of practical wisdom. She represented income. How could curiosity about what was going on in Cy's office compete with that? But Tuttle had extensive and inaccurate knowledge of the hunches that had led to the great breakthroughs in science, in the arts, in sports. Playing his hunch, he waited until he saw Vivian go by on the way to her office, pushing her machine. A minute later he followed.

Vivian looked at him suspiciously when he came into her office, where she was hooking up her machine, doubtless getting ready to transcribe what she had taken down in Horvath's office.

"Who is he?"

She tipped her head to one side and pursed her mouth.

"The man whose deposition you took down."

"It wasn't a deposition. He just told a long story. Most of it sounded like bull to me, not that I listened very carefully."

"What's his name?"

"Flanagan." Vivian brightened. An Irish name.

"I know Flanagans. I never saw him before."

"He's been away."

"What's his first name?"

Vivian had to check. "Wallace."

Tuttle laughed.

"It's a perfectly ordinary name."

Vivian and Peanuts made a pair, a pair of deuces. It was pretty obvious that Vivian had no idea how impossible what she was saying was. He wanted to tell her that Wally Flanagan was dead. No doubt this guy was an impostor hoping to benefit from recent events. He thanked Vivian and left.

For the second time that day, he ran into Peanuts in the rotunda.

"You wanted to know what's going on. Wally Flanagan is back," Peanuts said.

"And Hazel is the queen of Romania."

Peanuts seemed undecided how to take this.

"You got a car, Peanuts?"

"Where we going?"

"The Loop."

"Why should I?"

"Friendship?"

Peanuts seemed touched. He led the way to his car and, when they were settled in, said, "Is she really Roumanian?"

* * *

At the building, when Sandra asked him to come up, Tuttle left Ferret and Peanuts discussing Chinese restaurants in the locality. Unlike the elevator in the courthouse, this one rose silently and swiftly. Sandra was in her open doorway when he emerged from the elevator.

"Have you heard?" she asked.

"Tell me in your own words," Tuttle said and breezed past her into the elegant apartment.

"When I was visiting my father, Maud got a call from someone who said he was Wally Flanagan. She would remember him from the monastery. He wanted her help in breaking the news to his father."

Tuttle took off his tweed hat. "So you've already heard."

The reappearance of Wally Flanagan occupied the attention of Phil Keegan and Cy Horvath, but Agnes Lamb's thoughts were on the body that had been found in a Flanagan cement mixer and identified as Wally's. She drove out to Flanagan Concrete. The whole area was fenced. She crossed the lot and went up the steps and into the reception area. There was no one behind the counter that cut the room in two, but there was a bell to ring. She rang it.

From an inner office came the sound of a frantic voice. "What the hell do you mean they're not ready? How long do they think we can drive around before we pour?"

Whatever answer he got did not satisfy him. A loud expletive accompanied the slamming down of the phone. Agnes rang the bell again.

"What!"

She waited, and soon a man came out of the inner office and scowled at her.

"Who's in charge here?"

"Who are you?"

She displayed her ID.

He came to the counter, took it, and studied it, comparing her with the photograph. "You a parole officer?"

"Are you on parole?"

He thought about it, then smiled. "Frank Looney." He thrust out his hand. "How can I help you?"

"I want to ask you a few questions."

His phone was ringing. "Now?"

"Go ahead, answer it."

"Thanks a lot." She went around the counter and followed him into the office. The call brought good news, apparently. He turned from the desk and seemed surprised to see her there. "Have a seat. What's it about?"

"Murder."

He had been in the process of sitting down but paused in midair before dropping into his chair. "Murder?"

"It's an old case, of course, but now that Wally Flanagan has come back from the dead . . ."

"What!"

"You haven't heard?"

He hadn't. She gave him a brief version.

He listened with his mouth open, gripping the arms of his chair. "Jesus."

"It is sort of like Easter."

"You really mean it, Wally's back?"

"Which makes the body that was discovered here and identified as his a bit of a puzzle."

He was still stunned by the news that Wally had reappeared. Agnes remembered that Frank Looney was Wally's cousin and Luke's nephew. Maybe she should have been more subtle, but if he was surprised to hear of the reappearance, she was equally surprised that he hadn't already known of it.

"So what can you tell me?"

"What can I tell you? Nothing new. You must have records on it. Why waste my time? Look, I want to call my uncle."

"Go ahead."

"I mean I don't have time to reminisce about a body found years ago." He pulled the phone toward him and began punching numbers, then frowned at her and turned away.

Had he expected her to go? Agnes didn't like the thought that the unknown victim would end up as an unimportant footnote to Wally's return.

He had got through to his uncle. "Luke, what's this about Wally?" Pause. "No, I hadn't been told. What the hell's the secret?" He looked over his shoulder at her, the phone pressed to his ear. "All right, all right." Then, "What great news." He sounded like a man who had been told the good news that those who had firebombed his house had been apprehended. An old *Mad* magazine joke. He hung up. He looked around the office as if he hadn't noticed it for a while. Portrait of a man thinking. He stood.

Agnes did not. She was remembering Luke's irate visit to Robertson. "It sounds like a Pianone job."

This got his attention. "What are you talking about?"

"The body in your cement mixer."

"For crying out loud."

"I wonder whose it was."

"Go dig it up and find out!"

Not a bad idea. Agnes did get up then. He followed her through the door. There was a very large girl behind the counter now. She looked at Agnes, seemingly wondering how she had got into the inner office.

"I have to leave, Myrtle," Looney told her. "Everything's under control. Call my cell phone if anything comes up."

"Yes, Frank."

Ah, the devoted receptionist, spending her days behind these dusty windows, entertaining fantasies about the moment her boss would look at her as if for the first time, and . . . Well, she would be difficult not to notice, size-wise.

Frank Looney pushed through the door and outside. Belatedly he thought to hold it open for Agnes. He stood for a moment, looking around, surveying his little kingdom. He turned to her and tried to smile. "This hits me pretty hard, you know."

"Good news is like that."

He thought about it, then nodded, skipped down the steps, and headed for a dusty car.

Agnes watched him go, then went back inside. "How long have you worked here, Myrtle?"

"What business is that of yours?"

Again she got out her ID.

"Ten years."

"Wow. You must have worked for Luke Flanagan."

"He hired me, yes. Frank kept me on when he took over."

"I didn't realize he hadn't heard about his cousin."

Neither had Myrtle. She listened, her blue eyes sparkling in their pouches.

"No wonder he's upset."

"How so?"

"He has the job Luke wanted his son to have. But Wally thumbed his nose at the idea, and Luke let him, made him a rich man."

Did she think that Wally had returned to take over Flanagan Concrete? "So you've been here ten years."

"It's a job."

"Is Frank married?"

"Sure, to the business." She pursed her mouth.

"You must have been here when that body was found in the mixer."

She rolled her eyes. "To think it wasn't Wally after all."

"I wonder who it was."

"I don't. There are some things it's wise not to wonder about."

"Did the Pianone deal fall through?"

"Deal? There was no deal."

"Luke quashed it?"

"Thank God. I'm not sure I would have stayed here if there was any connection between that family and Flanagan Concrete."

"I wonder if there wasn't already a connection."

Marco just looked at her stone-faced when he heard about Wally Flanagan.

"I didn't think he'd dare to come back," Sylvia said. She studied the photograph that was captioned THE BEARDED PRODIGAL. "I like the beard."

Well, with her blond crew cut, Wally would find her different, too. Northern Minnesota was so long ago now that Sylvia could remember only the good part. At first it had been a vacation in a strangely beautiful place, the trees, the lake, the enormous sky above at night. Television reception was lousy, but that hadn't mattered, at first. Wally was content to fish and read, and Sylvia just took it easy. There wasn't much to do in the town where Sylvia did the shopping. For any excitement, you had to drive to Bemidji. Wally hadn't wanted excitement. Besides, he didn't want to run the risk of someone recognizing him, improbable as that was. Sylvia wondered if anyone else from the Chicago area was dumb enough to bury themselves in the woods of northern Minnesota.

Sylvia had made a lot of shopping trips to town, just to get away. There was a bar, the Rainbow, on the road that ran along the lakefront; it was the local favorite, always full of people, lots of fun. She could be gone for hours, and when she came back Wally seemed hardly to have noticed she'd been away.

"We're not staying for the winter, are we?"

"Sylvia, this is home now."

"Ask someone what winter is like here."

"It can't be any nicer than the other seasons."

"Wally, they have snow up to their gazoo. We'll be stranded here."

If she had thought it was temporary, he clearly regarded it as permanent. It became a constant theme.

"God, how I nagged him."

Marco grunted. "I told you it wouldn't work."

"You did not. You never say a word."

"You might do likewise."

"Whose body was it?"

"Don't ask."

The afternoon she met Greg Packer in the Rainbow, winter had come and gone too many times. He squeezed in next to her. "Hi."

"I've never seen you here before."

"I just got here."

"From where?"

"How's Wally?"

"Who's Wally?" Her first thought was *Now we'll have to get out of here. Someone knows who he is.*

"We grew up together."

They moved to a table. He was a good-looking guy, but he didn't seem as old as Wally. Boyish. How had he known where Wally was?

"We came up here one summer when we were kids. Well, eighteen, nineteen. Hitchhiked all the way. It's where I would have headed if I wanted to disappear."

So she took him back to the cabin, leading the way, keeping an eye on him in the rearview mirror to make sure he made the turns. At the cabin, she waited beside her car until he got out of his, then led him inside.

"Surprise!"

Wally was in his Barcalounger in what he called the supine position, a book on his belly. He didn't seem at all surprised. "Greg." He put out his hand. "Welcome to the woods."

There were times when Sylvia wondered how accidental Greg's arrival was. She could imagine Wally summoning his old friend to take her off his hands. If that was the plan, it worked. With Greg settled in at the cabin, Sylvia had someone to do things with.

When Wally left, it wasn't jealousy; he was as tired of Greg as he was of her. They were like kids after he left and had a whee of a time. Once there was nothing to prevent her from getting out of the woods, she found herself liking it there, or at least not hating it as she had. It was later, when she and Greg had returned to Fox River, that it became clear that Wally's departure had been part of an agreement. Greg was curious about her money, no doubt about that, but he had money, too. From Wally.

"I promised to do him a favor."

The favor was to provide proof positive that Wally Flanagan

was no more. The question was how to do that. The agreement had not been specific.

Packing to leave the cabin, she had found the wedding band in the drawer of a bedside table. She looked at it and then dropped it into her purse. When she told Greg, he lit up. "Let me see it." He turned it over and over with a thoughtful look. "You know, I was best man at their wedding."

The idea was to slip the wedding band on some dead man's finger and have him identified as Wally.

Sylvia thought it was a crazy scheme. "His wife would have to identify the body."

"You're right."

They had both grown up in Fox River, so, of course, their thoughts turned to the Pianones. They would know how to arrange something like this.

Wally Flanagan's mention of Sylvia provided a spoor that Agnes decided to follow, and that was how she found out that the woman was back in Fox River and hooked up with Marco Pianone. Agnes was in the lobby, talking with Ferret, when Sylvia swooshed out of the elevator and glided toward the front door.

"Sylvia!" Agnes called, and the gliding stopped. She looked at Agnes, who was not in uniform, puzzled. Her eyes switched to Ferret, who lifted his arms in a protest of innocence. Sylvia pushed through the revolving door, and Agnes followed.

"Where can we talk?" Agnes demanded.

"Who are you?"

"Do you want to see my police ID, right here in front of everybody?"

They went to the Starbucks in the next block. Agnes identified herself. "How's Marco?"

"That goddam doorman."

"Once they start talking, they can't stop."

It helped that Sylvia thought she knew more than she did. Getting the conversation onto Wally Flanagan proved to be a good move.

"He mentioned me?"

"That's why we're talking."

"What did he say?"

"About you?" Agnes smiled mysteriously. "Life in the woods sounded pretty nice."

"Oh, he loved it. And it was nice. Not much happening, you understand, but peaceful."

"So why did he leave?"

Sylvia made a face and sighed. "Men."

"In the plural?"

Sylvia stared at her for a moment. "He mentioned Greg?"

"Tell me about that."

It was a strange story. Sylvia seemed able to transfer her affection easily from one man to another and still retain the thought that she was true blue.

"And now Greg is dead."

Sylvia became wary. For the first time, she seemed to realize that she was blabbermouthing to a cop. She pursed her lips.

"We're worried that you could be next."

"What!"

"You must pose as much of a threat as Greg Packer did."

Her widened eyes were full of the sequence of thoughts Agnes's remark had caused. After a minute of silence, she said, "Where could I hide?"

"Don't worry about that. We'll protect you."

"That's a laugh."

"You're not laughing."

It took twenty minutes to convince her that she had to get out of the apartment. No need to mention Marco. Who knew Marco better than she did?

Agnes went to the apartment with her and helped her pack. One huge suitcase and a garment bag did it. Then Sylvia stood, looking around wistfully.

"The furniture yours?"

"Who knows? Let's go."

In the lobby, Ferret was all eyes, but only Agnes looked at him. He didn't seem all that broken up about losing this tenant.

Back in Fox River, in an interrogation room, Sylvia sang like a bird, but she kept coming back to Wally, wanting to know what he had said about her.

"You make an indelible impression," Agnes said.

"Sometimes I wished we had just stayed there, in Minnesota."

"Tell me about Marco and Greg."

"I had no part in it. It was a deal Greg had made with Wally, and when he found out about me and Marco, he saw a way to do it."

What she did know was that Greg had talked with Marco and later a body identified as Wally's had been found, in pieces, in one of the Flanagan cement mixers.

"Where can I go?"

She had mentioned Brenda Kelly, and Agnes wondered if Sylvia's old friend might not be the temporary solution to Sylvia's problem.

Cy Horvath, who had been monitoring the interrogation through the one-way mirror, said he would talk to Brenda. "Good work, Agnes." Still, he seemed less than happy about what she had discovered.

The unhappiness was general. Phil Keegan scowled and shook his head. "The Pianones."

The only Pianone Agnes knew was Peanuts, and she did not share the assumption that the Pianones were untouchable. Regardless, the decision was to keep quiet about what they had learned and wait on events.

"What events?"

"We'll see what Marco does when he learns he has lost his bimbo."

Days went by, and Marco did nothing. Meanwhile, Agnes got to know Ferret better.

"Where'd she go?" the doorman asked.

"Who?"

"Come on. You moved her out of here."

"What was she like?"

"Don't ask me. She never talked to me." He began to talk

about Sandra Bochenski. There was a real lady. She always stopped to talk to Ferret. "Even after her run."

"She runs?"

"Every day."

Jogging on the streets of Chicago among all the exhaust fumes did not seem the road to longevity to Agnes, even with that big lake blowing fresh air into the mix. Agnes was with Ferret when Sandra Bochenski, in street clothes, stopped by to ask why Sylvia didn't answer her phone. Ferret looked at Agnes.

"She moved," Agnes said.

"Who are you?"

Ferret answered. "A Fox River detective."

Sandra took a closer look. "I recognize you."

Agnes had sat in when Cy interrogated Sandra.

"Any other old girlfrends of Wally Flanagan's in the building?"

This was meant to annoy, but it didn't. "When are you going to find out who killed Greg Packer?"

"Any suggestions?"

"It wasn't Mr. Flanagan."

"That's good to hear."

Sandra had talked with Luke at the retirement home where he and her father and Maud lived.

"Have you talked with Wally?"

She thought about it. "I don't want to. I'm going back to California."

Ferret groaned, and Sandra patted his arm, causing the little guy to beam.

Marco never showed up. The man who did went through the lobby as if he knew where he was going. He took the elevator to the floor of Sylvia's apartment. He came down again in fifteen minutes. He started toward Ferret, looked at Agnes, then turned toward the door. No doubt he would take Marco Pianone the news of Sylvia's departure.

"So what are we waiting for?" Agnes asked, standing in front of Captain Keegan's desk.

"With the Pianones you never know."

"You mean we'll do nothing?"

"What would you suggest."

"Bring in Marco."

"Not yet."

Meaning not ever. Agnes left the office, mad. She ran into Peanuts and said, "How's your cousin?"

"Which one?"

"How many you got?"

"I'd have to count."

Did he know how?

Along came Tuttle. He doffed his tweed hat and asked, "What's up?"

"She's asking about my cousin."

Tuttle's expression changed. "Got to run," he said, and he did.

Everyone ran from the Pianones. On her way home, Agnes thought of that body that had been found dismembered in the cement mixer. She turned around and headed for Flanagan Concrete.

Frank Looney wasn't in his office. She asked Myrtle if she knew where he had gone.

"He said he went to see a priest."

When Marie Murkin looked into the study to tell Father Dowling that Frank Looney had come to see him, she added in a whisper, "It's his real name."

"Where is he?"

"In the front parlor."

He went to the parlor to find a seated Frank Looney staring out the window.

The visitor got to his feet when Father Dowling came in. "I'm Wally's cousin."

"Ah."

"I'd like to see him."

Father Dowling could have just said that Wally was back in his father's house, in the garage apartment, but instead he asked Frank Looney to sit. The priest took a chair behind a desklike table.

"I manage Flanagan Concrete."

"So I've been told."

"It's what my uncle wanted Wally to do. When he refused, Luke put me in charge."

"I know a Jesuit named Looney."

"My brother."

"You haven't talked to Wally yet?"

"Why did he come back?"

"I had better let him tell you that."

"What's the secret? Look, I've been thinking, Father. If he's changed his mind, I'll step aside. I've already told Luke."

"That's very generous of you."

"Luke is the one who's been generous."

"He seems very pleased with you."

"He said that?" Looney seemed genuinely surprised.

"His only criticism was the Pianone matter."

Looney lifted from his seat and then collapsed back into it. "Of course he was right. I was a damned fool. I guess I thought if my family could change, so could the Pianones. It made sense that they would want to invest in a legitimate business. Until you thought about it, that is. No, it was stupid on my part. I learned my lesson."

"You don't think the Pianones have changed?"

His eyes drifted away. "Wally had the right idea. I'd like to just disappear, the way he did."

"To a monastery?"

"Away from Fox River."

Father Dowling told him then that Wally was no longer staying at the rectory.

"Where is he?"

"He's gone home."

Looney was on his feet.

"He's staying in that apartment over the garage."

Wally no longer looked like a vagrant, although he had kept

the beard. He was surprised that he could wear clothes he had worn years ago, but there was no way he could move back into the Flanagan house with Melissa living there. There had been no reunion. They had talked, but whatever had passed between them was not something Wally wanted to reveal.

"Of course, she's right. I never expected it could be the way it was."

Marie had reacted by expressing the fear that they had a permanent guest in the rectory. It was his father who suggested the garage apartment.

"They have to get used to one another," he said to Father Dowling. "All those years he was away . . ." His voice drifted off, as if Wally had been overseas with the army rather than living in isolation without any apparent concern for the wife he had abandoned. Luke clearly thought the couple would eventually reunite.

"What did he want?" Marie asked when she found that Looney had left the rectory.

"He wondered if we had a spare guest room."

"Any more of that and you can get someone for my apartment."

"I can't have that sort of thing going on in the rectory, Marie."

The turn events had taken cast gloom over Phil Keegan. He chewed on an unlit cigar and glared unseeing at the television screen, where a semblance of baseball was being played by the Cubs. Everything they had learned pointed to the Pianones, and that meant impasse. Sylvia had told Agnes Lamb that Greg Packer had consulted Marco Pianone for help in carrying out his promise to Wally to stage his death and thus free him forever from his past. The mangled body in the Flanagan cement mixer seemed the obvious result of that collaboration. The wedding ring that had been the basis of Melissa's identification of the body had been brought from the cabin in Garrison.

"Have you talked with Marco?"

Phil's scowl deepened. This obvious move was one he could not make. If he did, the chief, Robertson, would intervene. There was even the possibility of demotion, and then who would run the detective division? No doubt someone with no scruples at all about the dominance of the Pianone family. Phil's decision not to proceed thus looked to be the choice of the lesser of two evils.

"Where is Sylvia?" The question sounded like a line from a poem.

"Agnes stashed her with an old friend. Brenda somebody. The two of them worked for Wally years ago."

Clearly Agnes and Phil thought that the woman was in danger. If the death of Greg Packer pointed to the Pianones, and if the woman Sylvia had been the one who linked the two, she might well be silenced in the way Greg Packer had been.

If Phil was despondent, Cy Horvath, for all his impassivity, was even more so. One afternoon, he came to the kitchen door, and Marie, after unsuccessfully trying to discover what the purpose of the visit was, came to tell Father Dowling that Cy was in the kitchen.

Cy wanted to talk, and Father Dowling suggested they go outside, much to Marie's annoyance. How could she eavesdrop from a distance? They sat on a bench just outside the sacristy door, under a walnut tree. Before sitting down, Cy picked up one of the green walnuts that littered the lawn. They sat in silence for a time, and then Father Dowling said, "Phil is feeling pretty low."

Cy shrugged. "Wally solved the big mystery of his disappearance, and Sylvia gave us the solution to the death of Greg Packer."

"And you're stymied?"

"The Pianones."

"The untouchables."

This explanation of Greg Packer's death made the famous trapdoor ladder irrelevant. If Greg had relied on Marco, the man's appearance at the garage apartment would not have caused him concern and he would have admitted his murderer unawares.

"The wrench?" Father Dowling said.

Cy turned to him and almost smiled. "Just what I've been thinking. How did he get hold of that? It came from the bench in the garage. All the tools were very carefully stowed, a place for each. A missing place from which the wrench had come."

"And only Marco Pianone can explain that?"

Cy grunted. "Or why he risked a daytime visit to the Flanagan house. The Pianones don't take risks like that."

"You think he might have been seen?"

"Agnes looked into that." He tossed the walnut, and it bounced along the walk. "Not that an identification would matter."

Every avenue seemed blocked by the power of the Pianones.

"Agnes Lamb thinks we're cowards. She's right. But what good would courage do? Even if we brought Marco in, nothing would follow. He wouldn't tell us anything; Robertson would go ballistic; Phil and I would be back on a beat."

"Maybe a good soluble crime will come up." It seemed hollow consolation.

"That's the only thing that could distract Agnes."

"What do you mean?"

"She's still pursuing it. Phil absolutely forbade her to approach Marco, so she is concentrating on Flanagan Concrete. Her idea is, if she could find unequivocal evidence of Marco's involvement in putting that body in the mixer, we would have to proceed."

It was clear that Cy admired Agnes's tenacity, however doomed to frustration it seemed. When they stood, Cy made a soccer kick at one of the fallen walnuts, and it sailed twenty yards onto the lawn.

"This can't go on, Father," Luke Flanagan said when he telephoned. "There she is in the house, and he's in the garage apartment. They really haven't spoken to one another yet."

"Give it time."

Luke took hope from this. "You think they'll get back together?"

"Stranger things have happened." What a reservoir of inanities he seemed to have.

"Would you talk to them, Father? All they need is a boost."

Who could blame the old man for hoping that the weird events of recent years could terminate in the status quo ante, his son back with his wife, everything as it had been? Greg Packer seemed not to enter into Luke's thoughts. Reluctantly, Father Dowling agreed to talk to Melissa and Wally.

When he got to the house, he found that Luke and Maude Lynn were also there. Had Luke wanted to be on hand for what he hoped would be the great reconciliation? Melissa took Father Dowling onto the sunporch, which was filled with potted plants.

"Some of these go back to my mother-in-law." It was an odd thought, a woman's plants living on years after she was dead.

Father Dowling feigned interest. "What kind is this?"

She laughed. "It's called mother-in-law's tongue." There were little spikes at the tips of the long tonguelike leaves. Whatever neologisms botanists devised, they did not replace such traditional names for plants.

"What do you think of Maud, Father?"

"What should I think?"

"I think they'll marry."

"That's not the marriage that is uppermost in Luke's mind."

She looked away. "I know."

"You should talk to Wally."

She bristled. "Why doesn't he talk to me? There he is, out there in that garage apartment, and he can't bring himself to come to the house."

"Would you want him to?"

Again she looked away. "I don't know."

"You have to realize how guilty he feels."

"Poor Wally!"

"I'm going to talk to him."

"Please give him my regards."

"I will."

The last time Father Dowling had been in the garage apartment, he had given conditional absolution to Greg Packer. He climbed the stairs and found the apartment door open. Wally was at ease in a very comfortable-looking chair, reading. He looked up, unsurprised, when Father Dowling said hello.

"Dad said you'd be coming." He put a marker in his book.

"What are you reading?"

Wally held up the book. It was *The Kreutzer Sonata* by Tolstoy.

"A pretty grim story."

"Life can be grim."

"Your cousin Frank came to see me."

"He told me. He was here." A wry smile. "He actually thought I had come back to replace him at Flanagan Concrete."

"And you reassured him."

"I don't know. He talks about getting away. Doing what I did."

For the first time, it occurred to Father Dowling that Frank Looney was in as much danger from the Pianones as Sylvia was. Marco must have arranged with Frank for the body to be found in one of the Flanagan mixers.

"What's he got to run away from? Dad says he's been doing a great job managing the business."

Father Dowling decided to tell Wally the explanation the police had hit on of Greg Packer's murder.

Recalling the grisly deed that had been done there seemed to alter the aspect of the apartment. As he listened, Wally looked around as if seeing the place for the first time. "Frank wouldn't sit down when he was here. Just paced up and down, looking at everything, checking the cabinets in the kitchen. He acted as if he had never been up here before, but, of course, he must have been thinking of what happened to Greg."

"He had been here before?"

"Oh, sure. When we were young. There was talk of him living here after I was married. Maybe if he had, I wouldn't have become involved with Sandra in the first place." He shook his head. "What a thoughtless guy I was. Just a stone's throw from my father's house."

"Frank might have been involved when Greg decided on the way to fulfill his promise to you."

"What promise?"

"To stage your death."

Wally seemed genuinely puzzled. "I don't know where he got that idea. Believe me, when I heard I was dead it was the surprise of my life."

"You mean the way Greg did it?"

"When I heard, I didn't know he was involved."

"How did you expect him to arrange it?"

"Father, there wasn't any arrangement. Why Greg did it, I don't know, but it was his own idea."

"But your wedding ring."

"He must have found it in the cabin at Garrison. The place in Minnesota. Of course, I had stopped wearing it."

"You didn't ask him to stage your death?"

"No."

"Then why . . ."

Wally thought about it. "Maybe it had something to do with his relationship with Sylvia. She had quite a nest egg. I had seen to that. With me definitely out of the picture, or seemingly so, the coast was clear for him."

"But she was mixed up with Marco Pianone."

"She was never a good judge of men." Another wry smile.

One piece of the theory as to how Greg Packer had died had to be rejected, but that left the theory intact. What difference did it make whether or not Greg was fulfilling a promise to Wally? It was what he had told Sylvia, but Wally's suggestion about Greg's designs on Sylvia's money, given his previous track record in California, made sense. In any case, Greg had arranged with Marco Pianone for a dismembered body to be found in a Flanagan mixer with Wally's wedding ring as basis for identification. Greg had paid the price of his association with the Pianones, and Sylvia remained vulnerable. So did Frank Looney.

Father Dowling spent a sleepless night, unable to drive from his mind the sequence of events that had led up to the murder of Greg Packer. At two in the morning, he went down to the kitchen and heated some milk. He sat at his desk in the study, sipping it, hoping sleepiness would come. What came instead was the thought that Phil Keegan's theory was all wrong.

Agnes Lamb knew that Phil Keegan was humoring her, tolerating her, but as an African-American woman she had a lifetime of experience handling that sort of thing. What she needed was an end run. She sought out Peanuts and found him in the courthouse pressroom, dozing, while Tuttle was needling Mervel for his cowardice in not writing the real story of Greg Packer's death. Agnes took a chair. Maybe this was the end run she was looking for.

"What good is the freedom of the press if you don't use it?" Tuttle asked the reporter.

"I don't want to end up in a cement mixer."

"Mervel, you'd end up in bronze. Public opinion is the only real weapon in a democracy."

"They wouldn't publish it."

"You don't know that."

"I don't know Singapore either, but I know it's there."

"Tuttle's right," Agnes said.

Tuttle turned, delighted with this support.

Peanuts came awake with a snarl. "What's going on?"

"We're talking about your family," Agnes said.

Peanuts struggled to his feet, glared at Agnes, and shuffled out of the room.

"He'll report this," Mervel said, his voice tremulous.

"He was sleeping."

"You told him we were talking about his family."

"With his IQ, why worry? Let me tell you what we're going to do."

Tuttle pulled his chair next to hers as she outlined the plan she could almost believe she had thought of before coming to the pressroom.

"I've been out to Flanagan's, I've talked to Looney, but we never really looked into what happened there."

"That was years ago."

"Looney was involved. And there's a woman, a receptionist named Myrtle. She has to know something, or at least have some idea of how it was done."

"Whose body was it?"

"The best guess is some vagrant."

"Who donated his body to crime." Tuttle was pleased with his remark.

"I doubt that he was a conscious participant."

"What a way to go," Mervel said.

"Exactly. It adds to the horror. My God, what a story."

Mervel's eyes filled with visions of grandeur, the intrepid reporter who defies the local crime family to satisfy the public's right to know. Agnes noticed his change of attitude. What he needed was stiffening up.

They adjourned to the bar across the street, where Mervel ordered a martini. "I hate martinis."

"Order something you like."

"This way I won't overdo."

Agnes would not have wanted to know what Mervel considered underdoing. He was on his sixth drink before he had the courage needed to put the plan into action.

She signed out a car, and the three of them were on their way to Flanagan Concrete.

It was the end of the lunch hour when they arrived, pulling into the yard behind Myrtle.

Agnes parked next to her. "Myrtle, I want to talk to you."

Tuttle helped Mervel out of the car. He steadied himself by putting a hand on the roof of Myrtle's car.

Agnes opened the passenger door and slipped in beside Myrtle. "I'd rather talk to you here than downtown."

"What do you mean?"

"I'll ask the questions. I want you to make an effort to remember what happened before that mangled body was found in a Flanagan mixer."

"Oh my God."

"You do remember that?"

"How could I forget? But what's the point of dredging all that up? It's water over the dam." And yards and yards of cement had been poured since.

"That truck still here?"

"I don't want to talk about it."

"Of course you don't. It must be a horrible memory."

"Did I say I remember anything?"

"Myrtle, how could you possibly forget?"

Agnes had lowered the window beside her, and Tuttle, tweed hat pushed back, stuck his head halfway inside. "I think that's Father Dowling's car." He nodded his head at an old Toyota.

"Why?

"For one thing, there's a prayer book on the front seat."

Myrtle pushed open the driver's door, and Agnes didn't stop her. Maybe it would be better to continue the conversation in the office. Agnes glanced into the car next to hers. Sure enough, a fat prayer book with ribbons trailing from it. As they crossed to the office building, Mervel zigzagged like a ship dodging mines. Tuttle helped him up the steps to the entrance.

Inside, Myrtle stopped and nodded toward the closed door of the inner office. "I didn't think he was here," she whispered.

"How do you know he is?" Agnes said, not whispering.

Myrtle sat at her desk, picked up the phone, and pressed a button. Her head cocked as she waited. And waited. Finally she put down the phone.

"He's not there?"

"He doesn't answer."

"Shall we continue?"

9

The morning after his sleepless night, Father Dowling wondered how to proceed with the thought that had occurred to him in the pellucid hours before dawn. Once he questioned the basis for Phil Keegan's theory, events took on an entirely different look. He considered talking with Amos Cadbury but rejected the idea. Putting it into words robbed it of much of the force it had in the realm of thought. All he had to do was imagine himself putting his thoughts before Phil Keegan to be dissuaded from that course. He could have spoken to Cy Horvath, but even that he hesitated to do. Meanwhile, the morning passed uneasily, and the time came for his noon Mass. Somewhere between the porch and the altar, his mind was made up. When he had finished saying Mass, he did not return to the rectory for lunch but went immediately to his car. Once he was under way, his conviction that he was on to something strengthened.

When he turned into Flanagan Concrete, the dusty air seemed a memento mori. He pulled into a guest spot in the parking lot, got out of the car, and stood looking at the mounds of sand and rock, the ingredients of the Flanagan product. If art imitates nature, cement retains the look of the natural materials of which it is fashioned. Not much activity in evidence, but then this would still be the lunch hour.

He mounted the steps and pushed inside to find a deserted reception desk. Beyond was an open door to an inner office. He stood for a moment, wondering if he had made this trip in vain, but calling to announce his coming would have deprived him of the element of surprise that might be essential. He went around the reception counter to the open door.

"Hello, hello."

The silence seemed to deepen. He looked into the inner office.

From a chair behind his desk, Frank Looney stared at him. "Father Dowling!"

He looked around. "I wanted to visit the scene of the crime." He laughed as he said it.

"Bit of a lull right now."

"Lunch hour."

Frank pointed at the Styrofoam container on the desk. "As you can see. What can I do for you, Father?"

"I think you can help me, Frank."

"Just say the word. Have a seat, have a seat."

Father Dowling sat. Again he looked around. "The police investigation into Greg Packer's death has run into an impasse."

"How so?"

"The Pianones."

Frank winced. "Please. Not when I've just eaten. So how can I help you?"

"It occurred to me that the impasse can be removed."

"Oh?"

"The explanation made sense. Then it occurred to me that it

makes sense even if the Pianones are left out of it. We still have that body found in one of your trucks."

Frank frowned in thought. "I'm not following you."

"Surely you must realize that suspecting the Pianones gives you protection in the matter? The assumption has been that you and Marco arranged for the identification of that body as Wally's."

"Now, wait a minute."

Father Dowling lifted a hand. "Say that you and Greg acted alone."

"Are you accusing me of . . ."

"Desecrating a body."

"That's ridiculous. Why would I do a thing like that?"

"Oh, any number of reasons, but the main one would be to seal your claim on your position here. With Wally definitively out of the way . . ."

"Wally's back."

"I don't imagine you counted on that. In any case, before his return, Greg represented a danger to you. It must have been uncomfortable realizing that your fate was in his hands."

Frank looked at him in silence, his expression now unreadable.

"Having gotten rid of Greg must have seemed pointless once Wally returned."

Frank laughed. "What a fantasy."

"It's the only explanation that makes sense. You knew of that entrance to the apartment from the garage below. Marco Pianone would not have known of that. You took the wrench from the tools over the workbench, lowered the ladder, and crept up to the apartment."

"I hope you haven't told this story to anyone else."

"I wanted to speak with you first."

Frank rose and stood for a moment behind the desk, picked up a roll of heavy tape as if he intended to wrap a package, and strolled toward the window. Father Dowling watched him. Any doubt he had had that Frank had killed Greg Packer was gone. The calmness of his reaction to the accusation was eloquent of guilt. Frank crossed the room and shut the door of his office. Father Dowling had to turn in his chair to look at him.

Frank shook his head, looking sad. "What am I going to do with you?"

"Oh, I suppose you could kill me, too. I wouldn't recommend that, however. You've already spoken of wanting to get away, just disappear as Wally did. I wouldn't recommend that either. His coming back proves that you can't run away from yourself. Of course, I understand why the thought would occur to you."

There was a long silence in the office.

"I've come here as a priest, Frank."

"You want to hear my confession?" He said it disdainfully, but then his expression changed. "That would silence you, wouldn't it?"

Father Dowling nodded. "It's your conscience you can't silence, Frank."

There were sounds in the outer office, and Frank looked wildly at the closed door and then sprang at Father Dowling, unreeling the tape as he came. He tipped over the chair in which Father Dowling sat, sprawling him on the floor. Before Father Dowling could get up, Frank was on him, wrapping the tape around his head and over his mouth. Father Dowling felt like a mummy as Frank pulled him to his feet and propelled him across the office and into an open closet, where he bound his hands and feet. As soon as the door shut, Father Dowling heard the voice of Agnes Lamb.

A slight noise from the inner office brought Myrtle to her feet. "What was that?"

Tuttle headed for the door of the inner office, but before he got to it the door opened and Frank Looney came out.

"What's going on, Myrtle?" He tried to smile.

Tuttle started again for the open door into the inner office, and Mervel went weaving after him.

"Where do you think you're going?" But Frank was not quick enough. Soon they were all assembled in the inner office.

Tuttle said, "Where is he?"

"What are you talking about?"

"Father Dowling. His car is in the lot."

"Who's Father Dowling?"

"Isn't he the priest you went to see?" Myrtle asked.

Frank glared at her as if he would like to strike her. Tuttle had picked up a roll of tape from the desk. He looked at Frank. Frank looked at him. Frank's gaze wavered, and Tuttle followed it. He turned, strode toward a closet door, and pulled it open. Father Dowling emerged like Lazarus. Tape clung to his head, wrists, and ankles.

Agnes put out a foot when Frank Looney tried to bolt from the office, sending him sprawling across the floor. Tuttle helped Father Dowling remove the tape, trying to take it easy where it was stuck to the priest's hair.

Meanwhile, Agnes had manacled Frank Looney. "What's the charge?" she asked Father Dowling. "Attacking a priest?"

"I'm afraid it's worse than that, Agnes."

"Greg Packer!" Tuttle cried.

Father Dowling nodded and went to Frank Looney and spoke softly to him. Frank swung his handcuffed arms at the priest, missing, losing his balance, and careening into Mervel. The startled reporter, in self-defense, grabbed hold of Looney's arms.

"Good work," Agnes said.

She called downtown before taking Frank Looney out and was advised to hold him there until help arrived.

"I've got help."

"Who?"

"Tuttle, Mervel, Father Dowling."

"Wait there," Cy Horvath said.

❧ Epilogue ❧

Jacuzzi, the prosecutor, swiftly obtained an indictment of Frank Looney for the murder of Greg Packer, aided by the interrogations conducted by Agnes and Cy Horvath, but even more by Frank's remorse of conscience. His confession could be admitted as evidence, of course, but it had hardly been needed. When a man who pleaded not guilty sat day after day in sight of the jury, haggard with guilt, taking little interest in the proceedings, while Tuttle strutted and fretted his hour upon the stage, his every intervention assuring Frank Looney's eventual conviction, even Jacuzzi could make short shrift of the matter. The guilty verdict, despite the relief it seemed to bring Frank Looney, caused no elation in the detective division. There had been no reference to the Pianones throughout the trial, and Mervel's pretrial bid for a Pulitzer was swiftly followed by an editorial correction and apology to the prominent Fox River family. A trembling and incompletely sober Mervel was dispatched to Marco Pianone to add his personal apology, after which he went on a three-day binge.

"Marco didn't kill Greg Packer," Phil Keegan told his subordinates, but he shuffled papers on his desk when he said it.

In the unused confession, Frank had reconstructed the murder: climbing into the apartment over the Flanagan garage by the ladder he remembered from years ago, carrying the wrench in his gloved hand. A startled Greg Packer had made a bolt for the stairway and been felled before he reached the door. Frank tossed the wrench down the stairs and then spent twenty minutes putting the apartment into apple-pie order for reasons he couldn't explain—he could not have left any prints of his own—and then exited as he had entered. Motive? He and Greg had loaded a vagrant who had been spending his nights sleeping in the yard of Flanagan Concrete into one of the mixing trucks after putting Wally Flanagan's wedding ring on his hand. The mixer had done its work, and there had been little left to identify. The ring had sufficed. But the gruesome deed had not brought the job security Frank had wanted.

The wedding service for Luke Flanagan and Maud Lynn was a subdued affair, but it brought out the denizens of the senior center in force. Wally and Melissa were on the altar with the mature couple, and their complete reconciliation seemed in prospect. Luke was as interested in the fate of the company he had founded as in the new life he was embarking upon.

"Sell," Wally suggested.

"To whom? The Pianones?"

"I doubt they'd want it now."

Wally was right about that. Amos Carbury offered to work with a Realtor while Luke and Maud were on their honeymoon, but Luke said he had another idea.

"Maud and I will live in the house," Luke announced. "I won't mind being boss again."

"Neither will I," said Maud.

The younger couple seemed to have as little interest in the house as Wally had in Flanagan Concrete. Earl Hospers promised to be the solution to that. Luke would resume the reins temporarily while he trained Earl to take over. Edna was ecstatic.

Marie Murkin was restrained at this news. "I suppose Edna will want to quit," she sighed.

"Oh, there's no danger of that, Marie," Father Dowling said. He turned to his visitor. "Would you like tea, Amos?"

"Is the pope German?"

"Marie."

Off to the kitchen Marie went.

"Phil Keegan and his department think the Pianones have gotten away with murder again, Amos."

"Perhaps with desecration of the body of that poor vagrant. The murderer of Greg Packer has been tried and convicted."

"Poor fellow."

"He seemed almost eager to be punished."

Punishment is always the hoped-for complement of crime, however seldom the two are combined. Rarer still is the criminal who admits his guilt. Wally Flanagan had returned repentant and was being welcomed back into the bosom of his family, the prodigal son returned, the mate of the putative widow forgiven, yet much of what had happened was the result of his perfidy. Sylvia and Sandra had gone off to California, taking Boleslaw Bochenski with them, an odd trio for that land of broken dreams.

Marie called them to the dining room, where the ritual of tea could be more fittingly performed.

Later, alone in his study, Father Dowling lit a pipe and thought long thoughts. Recent events had brought a renewed sense of the mystery of life. After a time, he took Dante from the shelf and found consolation in those measured cantos. *In la sua voluntade è nostra pace:* In his will is our peace.